DRAKON

Book I
THE SIEVE

C.A. CASKABEL

Contents

Join the Drakon Tribe.
Get the plunder

Join our newsletter to keep in touch with C.A. and win prizes. Those worthy (and lucky) will get their share of the loot! Prizes to be drawn:

- eReaders
- Drakon Paperbacks
- Fantasy e-books (you choose)

Click here to see to join this month's draw.

Join and Win

(http://caskabel.com/join)

A Note from the Author

About this edition: If you have never read Book I, then this note is irrelevant. Dive in, and I hope you'll enjoy.

If you have read Book I before July 2017: I decided to include the story of Sarah, the Apocrypha chapters, in this second edition of the book. This is the only change. Read it! It will reveal a whole different point of view.

I will not make any changes to Book II or III. Sarah appears again in Book IV, the final chapter of the story, due in late 2017.

Please take the time to rate and review this book. It is the only way to help a debut author.

Also, don't forget to check our giveaway on the previous page.

Thank you for reading.

C.A.

PS: Sarah "dreamt" and Da-Ren "dreamed." It is intentional.

www.caskabel.com

BOOK I: THE SIEVE

"I am Da-Ren, the First Blade of the Devil."

I.

Jar of Honey

Island of the Holy Monastery, Thirty-Second Summer.
According to the Monk Eusebius

"I am here to redeem the lives of my wife and daughter. I've brought the offering."

Those were the first words of Da-Ren, the man who would become my brother, hero, nightmare, savior, and my life's only story. He knelt and offered me an earthenware jar. Only moments earlier, he had crashed through the main cedar gate of our monastery, hurling his body against it. He had the eyes of an infidel, one whom God had not allowed to sleep for many nights. No one like him had ever set foot on our remote island of Hieros in the middle of the sky-blue sea.

Many a disheartened soul had climbed the thirty-eight and thousand more steps that led to the Castlemonastery. They came proud and strong on fast-moving triremes; they came humble and desperate on wave-ravaged fishing boats. They moored their vessels, whether great or small, in the eastern harbor and ascended to seek mercy or plead for a miracle. Cure for the incurable. Resurrection. Eternal life. God's kingdom is so often misinterpreted by the desperate.

Almost all descended the same steps one or two days later, some swiftly with wings of hope lifting their heels, others slowly with the look of a doom foretold in their eyes. And then there were those few who stayed at the monastery for a long time. They had found the strength to climb up but had lost what little was needed to climb down again.

On the day Da-Ren arrived, I was the novice monk in charge of the cleaning chores. I was airing the First Elder's chamber to rid it of the stench of the linseed-oil-burning lamps. A flash of movement caught my eye, and I looked out of the window through the spider web clinging to the limestone wall and the wooden shutters. A penteconter was slicing through the calm blue waters like a giant serpent, approaching the harbor's entrance. It was not a pirate ship; the swan carved on its stern was the mark of a merchant fifty-oared vessel.

A hide-clad man jumped into the sea with his boots still on before the ship was even moored. I clutched the wooden cross hanging around my neck. The man came ashore holding what looked like a jar with both hands above water, making his way across the razor-edged rocks. Biting my lower lip, I waited to see how many of his crewmates would follow. But none did. The man clambered over the salt-eaten stones without ever looking back.

I had counted several times, in the middle of a quiet day, how quickly someone could climb the narrow steps that led to our monastery. The young fisherman who often brought us fresh mackerel could climb the slippery steps barefoot before I counted five times a hundred. The barbarian was at the southwest bend, more than halfway from the shore, and I hadn't even reached twice a hundred.

As he approached, I could see the cross-shaped hilt of his sword, tied to his back. He was undoubtedly a man of the blade. One barbarian alone was enough to massacre the few aging monks of our commune, just as the searing wind had ravaged the last yellow flowers of spring.

This season full of earthly smells, the onset of summer, is often deceiving, for it is a season of raid and slaughter, the one that pirates choose to rip through both seas and virgins. Only one thing about this barbarian gave me the slightest bit of hope: the jar he carried with both hands as gently as if it were an infant.

I descended the coiled stone staircase from the second floor of the main building, with my long robe slowing my progress, and entered the courtyard. "The gate, shut the gate," I shouted.

My brothers were breaking their fast in the dining hall after the Morning Prayer, and the only one in the courtyard was deaf Elder Marcus, weeding the vegetable garden. I reached the gate just in time to meet eyes with the intruder, who was but five strides away. I managed to lock him out by securing the rusty latch, but there was no one to help me lift the wooden beam to seal the gate. Again and again came the thundering blows from the other side. The rotting wood shattered as his body crashed through, and his boot hit me high in the chest. I fell backward and hit the ground hard. Half hoping to ward him off, half making the sign of the cross across my chest, I raised an arm and begged, "Have mercy, in the name of God!"

He had the stature and the long, wavy brown hair of the Archangel, but he was dressed in the hides and boots of the pagan invaders, the barbarians of the northern steppe. The sharp lines of his face were forged as if the Devil himself had stretched a sheet of wheat-colored skin over bones of steel. It was the face of those bloodthirsty dogs sent by Satan and halted by God just above the Great River that, for centuries now, marked the natural borders of the Holy Eastern Empire. But not everyone found his face as terrifying as I did that day. In the villagers' settlement, beyond the Castlemonastery, many women would whisper his name for years to come when cold nights embraced them.

The man fell to his knees, his eyes watery, his brow sweating; he raised the jar and extended it toward me. To my surprise, he spoke his words in my tongue, that of Almighty God and his servants the Emperors: "Mercy. In the name of God. I am here…to redeem the life of my wife and daughter."

Each *r* rolled off his tongue like a boulder off a cliff. He grabbed me with his right hand, and my mind went blank from the pain as he pleaded, "Young man. Sorcerer of the Cross. Save us!"

Despite the strength of his hands and legs, he would be one of the few who had lost the will to ever leave this place again. He would stay with us until the very end. *Forever* is a word that I will not use, because I am a man of God, and it means other things to me. I dare not even utter the word, for that would imply that he failed in his mission. I never witnessed the end of his story. All I know is that he was the last to remain on Hieros many years later, that last summer morn when I and the rest of my fellow monks and villagers abandoned the island to save our lives and the silver and gold heirlooms from the pirates.

That first night, after the Compline Prayer, I brought the dark-green jar of his offering into my cell. Over the low heat of the candle, I burned the rope and removed the sailcloth that sealed the wide mouth of the urn tightly. I dipped my finger into the jar timidly, before curiosity became sin. Its taste was sweet but oddly foul on my tongue.

It was honey.

Sweet nectar of the immortal Satans from the dawn of time.

A chilling breeze whispered into my ear and crawled down my spine, the same way it does every time I read the *Dark Book of Our Faith* and the *Last Angels*. My eyes caught shadows crawling on the wall in the scant moonlight. The night birds, the demongirls. They disappeared as they came, diving in the lightless corners of the cell. I put my ear closer to the jar. I could hear them. The long, inconsolable wails of mourning emanating like fumes. It could have been just an aberration from my fiveandtenmore-day fast.

I placed the jar under the small shrine of the Holy Savior Maiden, our Mother of the Son. Her painted wooden icon was the most powerful amulet against all evil. Or so I thought back then. At dawn, they took the jar away from my cell.

This is the story of Da-Ren as I wrote it with my reed pen dipped in the ink, the black and the red. I buried it in a trunk in the dungeons of the closest monastery, on Foleron Island, to where I escaped.

I never saw the jar again.

Though I dreamed of it. Just the night before last.

II.
Puppy

Thirteenth Winter. The Sieve. First Night.

I am Da-Ren, the First Blade of the Devil.

I was born one night in the thirteenth winter of my life in Sirol, the big camp of the Tribe. Of the othertribal mother who bore me first, I will not say a word. It was fortunate for both of us that she died in childbirth.

On the rooster's second crow, the sound of a child's scream ended my sleep, and a sphere of light appeared through the horse hides that covered the tent's entrance. A monstrous shape entered with the torchlight. I could make out four hands and four heads, growling and searching. A strong hand grabbed my hair and started pulling me away from the warmth of the tent and my last night of child sleep, as if ripping me from the womb.

My left leg got caught on the dry, smoldering horse dung that fed the fire, and I cried out in pain. A burn mark remains on my calf to remind me that I once lived in the orphans' tents. The monster dragged me out of the tent and into the storm.

The first Demon of the world, Darhul the loathsome, spewed clouds of raven darkness from his nine heads, veiling the stars. Enaka, the One Goddess of the Unending Sky, cried rivers of tears that melted the earth below. She mourned her six sons, the six Suns who had perished during the ancient battle with the Demon. Selene, the shining silver heart of Enaka, was broken in half that night, cloaked with the cloudbreaths. Enaka hid her seventh son, her last precious Sun, for days, and at night she fought with her thunderbolts, flaming arrows of light, to drive the Demon back into his lair.

These were the Legends the old women of the Tribe poured into our heads every rainy, merciless winter. It was such a night, a night born of Legends, when the cowards pray for death and the brave rise fearless.

I crawled to get up, found my step, and then lost it again. The rain had started to fall at dusk, as sad and gray as the slobber of Darhul; the soil was kneaded into mud. I tried to slip away from the dark monster dragging me, but his fingers were coiled in my long hair. Just before my heart flew out of my throat, he shouted to me, "Shut up! Get up!"

He let my hair free, and I turned to face him. He was not a monster; he didn't have two heads. He wore a gray fur hat with black wolf ears. And there was a second man next to him. Both from my Tribe. I found hope. Old Man and Murky Eyes. Those were the names I gave them under the torch's light before I learned their real ones.

"In there, now!" Old Man shouted, showing me the wooden cage.

I turned to my right and broke into a run to escape. I hardly managed two steps before he kicked my foot. I lost my ground and splattered into the mud on my back. It was soft and cold, like defeat. He grabbed my head as if it were an apple and turned it to face him. I couldn't see the white of his eyes.

"You remember me, boy?" he asked.

I didn't make a sound.

"You're thirteen winters old. I spared you last winter. You weren't ready."

Old Man shoved me into the cage, head first. It was low, even for boys. I pushed the door with both hands, but it was too late. Old Man was locking the cage, and the other one was hitting the side poles with his club. Another pair of hands grabbed me from inside the cage.

"Da-Ren."

"Ughi."

"Malan."

Crawling. Touching. Feeling the cold hands and legs of the other children in there. A knee hit my jaw. I recognized their voices before their faces. Pale-faced Malan, Ughi the Puppy.

"Da-Ren, Da-Ren." Ughi held my forearm with both hands. He was shaking. "What's going on?"

I pulled away from him. I knelt and turned around, looking outside through the side wooden poles and the gray veil of rain. There she was. Her familiar eyes, fixed on me, gleamed outside the cage. She looked almost bald in the rain, the last wisps of white hair stuck on the wrinkled skin that covered her skull. Greentooth, the crone who raised me, was bidding us farewell.

"It's the Sieve, you cursed orphans. You'll be back here soon, scarred."

"The Sieve…" Malan whispered his first words.

The Sieve. The trial where the twelve-wintered became warriors. Of those the Sieve took every winter no one came back. I had wondered many times how and when a boy like me entered the Sieve. Those my age didn't know and the old crones would never say much about it.

"You don't prepare for the Sieve. It comes one night. The weak perish and the brave join the warriors," was all I had heard.

The Greentooth was humming: "Night's the Sieve, winter's Sieve…"

One of the men called, and the oxcart started moving through the mud, carrying the wooden cage with the three of us in it. I couldn't hear her anymore. Never again would I hear her voice. The wheels were wobbling through the heavy soil, and I felt each rock and puddle in my spine. It was a while before I started hearing other screams, some fading, some approaching. We were looking outside, searching for the men and the children moving in shadows.

"Who are these men?" asked Ughi.

"Guides. They gather the children for the Sieve every winter," said Malan.

"The one who grabbed me was so old," I said.

"Are they going to kill us?" asked Ughi, shaking.

"No, stupid," said Malan. He then turned to me and whispered: "Not yet. Not all of us."

As he finished his words, Old Man opened the cage. I pushed myself away from the door on my palms and heels. The Guides didn't take us out. Instead, they threw two more children inside.

"Atares of the Blades," said the first one as he entered. I saw his teeth first. He was almost smiling, awake, and ready for the trial of his life. "Are you all twelve-wintered here?"

Everyone nodded, even me. Atares wanted to talk. He wouldn't shut up for the rest of his life.

"Good. Everyone is twelve here; then this is the Sieve. Finally! You have names?"

"Yes. I am Da-Ren of the…" *Orphans.* I didn't say the word.

The second boy was growling, low, as they put him in, his fists punching the air. One of the punches landed on my arm, and I kicked him back. Atares got in the middle.

"Leave him; he is stupid. Urak of the Blades, they call him."

The boy was still growling, an ugly, drooling growl like a mauler, his eyes now wide open, now shut, as if he were waking in and out of a nightmare.

"Does he talk?"

"He is stupid even when he talks."

The oxcart was moving again. Atares pressed his cheeks against the wooden poles trying to see outside, to find the shadows within the rain. After a while, he started singing, still looking outside, his fists clenching the wooden poles.

Night's the Sieve, winter's Sieve,
part the grain from the weed,
night's the Sieve, winter's Sieve,
part the warrior from the weak,
part the Archer from the meat.

"Never heard this song," said Ughi.

"What? No mother to sing to you?" Atares mocked him.

"You know where we're from?" I asked.

"You orphans stink three tents away," he said, laughing. "Everyone knows where you're from."

I did stink. The previous afternoon, before the rain set in, the Greentooth had sent me to fill wooden buckets with fresh horse piss. Tanners used it to get the stench out of the freshly skinned hides. Colt or stallion, she said, not mare. That was my usual chore up until that day, to carry horse dung and horse piss. At dusk's light, as I was bringing in the last two pails, a war horse passing by me went into a panic. One step closer and it would have crushed me. The rider's leg kicked me down and the horse piss tipped all over me. Despite the downpour afterward, the stench was still on my skin. In whatever Sieve I entered, surely a better fate awaited me. If I lived.

Urak started kicking at the bars of the cage, and Malan punched him to stop.

"Shhh, I see lights," said Atares.

Tiny moons glowing brightly in the rain. As we got closer, I could see that they were torchlights under sheds circling a big clearing.

"That's the Wolfhowl," I heard Atares say. "Look around, see if there are any Witches. Look!"

The Wolfhowl of Sirol. The arena of the Ouna-Mas, the Tribe's Witches. Everyone except Ughi shifted near Atares to see.

"Is this…where they're taking us?" I asked.

Where the full-moon rituals took place. The sacrifices of the othertribers. I was not an othertriber. There was no full moon.

Atares broke the worried silence with a whisper: "Oh yeah, they take us to the firstborn servants of Darhul, the razortoothed Reekaal, as sacrifice. Those bloodeaters steal the weaklings and drown them in the night rains."

"You try to scare us with *this*?" Malan said.

The white-haired women had been telling us Reekal tales since the first winter I remembered myself. It would be scary had I been a seven-wintered. Or if they really took us out of Sirol, to the Forest, the lair of the Reekal.

We approached the torches outside Wolfhowl, but our cart didn't move in. Enaka the Golden Maiden pitied us and ordered the dead warriors resting next to her in the Sky to stop pissing on us. Silence fell like a second cloak of darkness as we waited there. A hooded man approached, his shadow outlined in the weak light. He stood next to the cage among Murky Eyes and Old Man and shouted, "To the Sieve!"

Our cart started moving again, away from Wolfhowl.

"That…was a Reghen, a Truthsayer," said Ughi.

"At last, you know something," Atares said. "Those Reghen are the tongues and the ears of the Tribe. They bring the words of the Khun, and the Ouna-Mas. Do you know who the Ouna-Mas are?"

I knew of the Ouna-Mas, the Tribe's Witches of untold birth, the only ones who spoke with the Goddess and the One Leader, the Khun.

We were heading west and north now, farther away from the orphans' camp. Toward the Forest. Dawn was a long way off. We went up a hill for a while until the oxen started to struggle to move the cart. Old Man was shouting and ripping the air with his whip, but we couldn't move a step. He opened the door of the cage, and he ordered us, "Get out. You go on foot from here. Follow him." He pointed to the second Guide who was leading, holding a torch under a hide.

We started running uphill until a jab of pain bit my side. I stopped to catch my breath. From the hill's top I looked back all the way to the orphans' tents. The sky was black, but the earth was full of fires, as if the bright stars of the brave had fallen to rest at our feet.

Down below us, more Guides were driving the oxcarts and cages up the hill. The torches etched the black earth with gold fire. Each cart alone was slithering away slowly like a flaming snake after devouring its prey.

"So many of them, more than a hundred," said Atares.

"What's a hundred?" Ughi asked. I wanted to ask the same.

"Look, Khun-Taa's tents. Down there." Atares pointed downhill to the center of Sirol where Khun-Taa, our Leader, and the Ouna-Ma Witches lived. West of them were the brightest fires of the Archers, the fierce horsemen. To the east of the Khun were the cutthroats, the Blades, and farther away the endless tents of the help: Fishermen, Tanners, Hunters, Blacksmiths, Trackers, and Craftsmen, all thrown together. Between the Blades and the Tanners were the few tents of the orphans. The asshole of Sirol. I would never cry for leaving that place, even if I had to go into the belly of Darhul.

"Move, don't stop."

A strong blow to the back and I was down again eating mud. It was soft and thick, like fresh shit. I got back up. We kept running, going down a much-trampled path. To the left of it were bushels of hay stacked under wooden sheds and behind them a prickly hedge bush as tall as I. To the right, only a few tents. The path led us to a small field. About ten breaths to run its length, its width twice that. A few sheds and tents around, the oaks gray skeletons in the west.

"Take off your clothes. There, next to the other children," Murky Eyes said.

Seven times the fingers of my one hand were the children. They were swarming around like crazed wasps that had their hive ravaged by a blazing torch. The Guides were pushing them to form a straight line.

"The first one to fall is finished!" shouted Old Man.

He then disappeared under the north shed to protect himself from the rain. More of those Guides stood there waiting, observing us. The Guides were covered in hides, wolf hats, and tall horsehide boots. We weren't.

"These men are so old, still alive," I said.

"Their rage is frozen, and their shame is heavy. The Tribe cast them out here to herd orphans under the storm. They don't like you, Da-Ren. Keep away from them," Atares said.

I pointed to the new shadows that were gathering. "Look at them. Archer boys."

"Shit, try beating them," muttered Ughi.

A tall Archer boy was running fast and eager toward us. He turned his head back and shouted triumphantly to the rest of his mates, "I told you! This is the westmost camp. Yeah. We are the best!"

There were a few girls among them too. The Guides brought one of them close to me, only Atares separating us. The torchlight shined strong on her face.

I know you. I've seen you.

Brown-haired, brown-eyed. Brown was the first color of the day.

"Westmost! Good. We're in a brave pack," I heard her voice.

I had seen her colors many times in Sirol. I was one of the few brown-haired boys, and the ravens always gave me spiteful looks. The fair-haired girls were favored and fortunate offspring of Enaka. But for a boy to have brown hair, it was a disgrace. All it meant was that my mother was a slave from the North.

"You're Elbia," I said.

She nodded, silent, a smile; a smirk? A smile. I had seen Elbia three times before. First, at the Archers' camp, one summer past. She was riding a brown mare, her hair and the horse's tail blowing in the wind in unison. Then three moons ago, at the bow trials of the eleven-wintered. She was faster than most boys on horse that day and stood out from all others, unlike me. We didn't practice with the bow a lot at the orphans. And then that same night when I fell asleep, in my dream; that was the third time.

I was in the same pack as Elbia. The boys who came with her were also from the Archers' tents. They had put me in a worthy pack. I smiled.

The cold night persisted, sucking the strength from the children like a ravenous bloodeater. Even the Archer boys fell silent. I was still searching for a stick to defend myself with. Some of the children were moaning already and wouldn't even raise their heads. Murky Eyes was shouting for silence. Silent tears. They stood like sheep, looking at the mud. None of those children who stood there, dead frozen, made it through the Sieve. At least, they didn't become Archers or Blades. Only the ones who disobeyed some of the rules managed to become warriors. The others would end up fishing bass and salmon from the great river, the Blackvein. They would make our tools and our boots. But they would never hold double-curved bows or blades, or own three horses each.

Ughi, that feeble orphan, would fall first. Or that other one, next to Elbia, the short, skinny girl with the curly hair. Her locks were coiled tight like newborn blackberry snakes when they brought her. As the rain fell heavily, her hair straightened and covered her back. The tall Archer boy five bodies down from me dropped to his knees. Murky Eyes covered the distance from the shed to the center of the field in a few quick breaths and waved his whip high. The boy managed to get back up, and with his head held low he pressed his arms on his half-bent knees to stay upright. Children in a row, pinned in the mud, trembling like willow trees on the banks of the Blackvein River. Barefoot, a loincloth around my crotch, a black silence without birdsong. My fingers and feet numb.

Ughi fell first. *Ughi, the puppy* we called him among the orphans. They had brought him there last winter from the Rods' tents when his mother died giving birth. Ugha-Lor was his name, named after Pelor the magnificent ancestor of men, but no boy ever used that. *Ughi, the puppy.* Weak legs, hollow cheeks. He usually smiled, as if he couldn't foretell his fate. He never managed to fight any of the other orphans for food. On some nights, he even lost his own share of gruel.

His legs melted fast, and he fell facedown.

"Get up," I whispered. "Kick him, get him up," I yelled to Malan, who was next to him.

"Get up, puppy."

Nothing.

Murky Eyes passed by me, made a grimace of disgust and murmured to himself before landing a thick gob of spit next to the boy's body. He touched Ughi on his bare back and then hugged him. From where I stood, they were two gray shadows embraced as one. The boy shivered, his legs kicked a few times, and the Guide held him tighter. The dark mud was a cold cloak.

"Puppy is freezing," I whispered to Atares.

"No, Da-Ren. It begins," he muttered, and he turned his eyes away from Ughi.

The Guide was stroking Ughi's hair. The boy wasn't kicking anymore. The sun found a break among the cloudbreaths and brought light and the first warm colors of the day. A deep dark red running down Ughi's neck. Death colored the mud darker. The Guide's blade caught the dawn's light. Children screaming. The only ghosts to ever haunt my nights. The Guide dragged the body a few paces in front of us so that we could all see. As he turned toward the shed, he whistled for the maulers.

There were two of them, two gray strong-necked dogs with drool glistening on their wrinkled jaws. The men of the South called them *molossers* and trained them for the battlefields. Our Tribe called them maulers. Easier on the tongue, and a more fitting name. The maulers charged without changing direction, the fastest going for the neck and the larger one straight for the meat. They didn't send the dogs for Ughi. He was already dead and wouldn't say a word as they ripped him apart. He liked dogs. He was the only one in the orphans who never tortured puppies. They sent the beasts to rip the spirit and the heart out of us.

It worked.

Apocrypha I.
My Name is Sarah

As the One Mother heard the Legends, Chapter I

Come noon, the sun's rays beam down the bottom of the dried-up well, and I see his grimy face staring up at me. He has been standing there, for six days and nights now; my brother's bloated corpse cuddled around his feet. It's the only way they both fit—the well is barely six feet wide—else he must step on the maggots and the wet rotting flesh of my kin.

Come night, I pray to the haloed angels to beat their milky wings and part the autumn clouds so that the moon can illuminate his screams. And when the angels listen—more often they don't—I have a second chance to see them both, the living and the dead next to each other. The moonlight paints everything in its own twisted magic, the savage's eyes are glowing mad and yellow; he still makes desperate efforts to climb up. To me. My brother's rotting face comes alive every time the savage tries to climb; the jaw gnawing at the leg of Jak-Ur. Maybe I dreamt that, I am not sure it happened, the light of the autumn moon is hazy and weak.

Jak-Ur is the name of the savage; it is one of the first words he taught me.

Water. Food. Help. Shit. Lift. Up. Jak-Ur. Sarah.

He said his name is Jak-Ur and I told him my name. He should know the name of his death.

We don't speak each other's tongue; we showed each other these words with hand signs, except for the word "help." That one he didn't need to sign.

"Fear."

We're both afraid, he of being trapped forever, me of him getting out—but how can I make a hand gesture for fear?

"Don't be afraid, sister," were my brother's last words.

I know now why we bury them fast, six days passed and the reek, oh Lord, the reek. I know now that once dead, the God's faithful stink as bad as the animals. And the color of his skin. Whatever is down there is not my brother anymore. It is dark and oozing and glistening—that might be the moonlight on the rainwater though—and doesn't have a face. Tiny ants creep down the stones at noon; fat spiders come up at sunset.

The well is made of gray stone. My father built it when he first came here, but it dried up a long time ago. We use it to dump filth, and dead kittens—not me, young Lonas, the woodcutter's boy drops the kittens. Poor Lonas, the savages took him, alive. Weeds have grown; they found some raindrops to suck and are extending between the stones of the circular well, flicking like lizard tongues that try to kiss both of them: the living and the dead. Truth be told, they are both dead, that they must know by now, the maggots may have eaten the flesh and the lips and crawl around the eyeballs of my brother, but that barbarous dog is dead too. He will live until I decide on the most painful death. I have thought of thirteen deaths so far, but it has only been six nights. I think I slept one night, I had dreams of rag dolls walking and wolves howling; they must come from sleep.

"Don't be afraid, little sister," my brother said; those were the last words I heard out of his mouth. Not the last sounds. That was squealing.

He spoke those words, his hand on my shoulder, a few moments after my father's slave, Agapetos, stormed among the huts screaming: "The dogs, the dogs. The infidels…coming." I was outside, washing, that's what they had me do most days. Washing clothes, the lye burning my hands until the priest comes to marry me; my father promised me to him. The wedding is supposed to be next month, before the holy winter night of death and birth, but I don't know anymore. I think it won't happen.

My father ran out of our hut, my brother right behind him, and asked Agapetos: "How many? How far?"

Agapetos, barely swerved his horse half circle and pointed backward. *Not far.* He then nudged the mare into a gallop and never looked back.

"Swords! Gather the men! Barricade behind the carts. Now, boy," were my father's last words.

Agapetos means "the one we love," how unfit for someone whom we have fed all his life, only for him to betray us, shouting "dogs" and then riding away. He didn't mean it as a curse. There were real dogs, black-skinned and strong-necked, and they reached before their masters, the riding archers. It was maybe four or five of them, but I heard them barking from far away. Only the last moment before they fell on our men did they go silent, focusing on the kill. And then came the flaming arrows, the riders, the scourge of God.

My father never had a chance to bravely wield his sword, a sword of the Empire, one he had carried around the battlefields victoriously, before the Emperor himself gave him land scrolls and appointed him two days south of the North River to grow the fields and defend the borderlands. How proud did my father sound every time he talked about the Emperor and his gifts. My mother was smarter than him.

The *boy*, my brother, fought bravely—if one can call what followed a fight—after my father fell. The rest of our men, fewer than ten among the huts, dropped fast, pierced by the arrows. The riders took Mother, they took Lonas, they took the women, and the very young. My brother was wielding his sword, surrounded by six riders, they were toying with him, poking him with their spears, until one of them, who must have been their warlord, the one on the rose-gray horse, shouted something in their barbaric tongue, and they turned and rode away. They had pierced him a few times, and a couple of the wounds were deep. Little brother fell to his knees, but he wasn't dead. The riders galloped away, all except for one. Jak-Ur. My brother had wounded Jak-Ur on his forearm; he managed to draw some blood from the dogs.

And then it starts and never stops, engraved in my mind forever.

Jak-Ur doesn't leave with the rest; he dismounts and approaches my kneeling brother. I am hiding in the empty oil barrel outside the barn. It has rotted, and the children use it to hide and play; they have opened holes to see through. I fit; I am slender and young, taller than a child, I make sure I am well-hidden in there, I pray that I am. I have to save myself, no Emperor or father will save me today.

My brother is bleeding out; his eyes dart desperately left and right.

Are you looking for me, brother? I am safe.

Jak-Ur punches my brother's face twice, sweat and blood and teardrops, and then grabs him by his long hair and starts pulling him toward the well. *Your last words I remember, but now I am afraid for you, little brother.* The words end but the sounds stay.

The sounds still come in the night; they haven't stopped for six days now. My brother fights as much as a wounded and long-defeated boy can fight. But he still fights, kicking and screaming, like…a girl. That's the words he'd use: "like a girl." Jak-Ur resolves to smash my brother's head on the top of the stone wall, the rim of the well that protrudes two feet above the ground. And then when brother is unconscious, or dead I hope, Jak-Ur puts brother against the stone wall, Jak-Ur is behind him, pulls down his pants, both their pants, and he starts thrusting back and forth, like the dogs and the stallions, and little brother's body just follows the motion, Jak-Ur pounds, little brother's face staring down the well, his bare legs and waist against the stones, and it never ends, a few moments to last a thousand years in my hell.

It is only the three of us left under the crimson and purple bleeding clouds—father's favorite colors, those of the Empire three-cut flags. The swirling autumn leaves whisper the last rites above the scattered corpses who don't want to see any of this and stay face down in the mud. I climb out of the barrel, I can't understand, believe, and I must get closer, to see my little brother. He is not my little brother, and I am not his little sister, we are twins of one womb sheath, and we look—we used to look—so much alike, everyone says that—Agapetos always did, and so did Mother. They took Mother. A man knocked her senseless and pulled her on a horse. She didn't see any of this; the priest always said that the

Lord is magnanimous. That he is, sometimes.

Jak-Ur spreads my brother's legs wider to have better support, and he steps on the stone ring. He can now rock faster and harder. Little brother always had his feet planted wide, father taught him so, to be a deadly swordsman, get in fighting position. When he turned eighteen last year, father gave him a sword and a hand-carved sheath. The empty sheath dangles shamed around my brother's waist, he has no pants, but the strap and the sheath are still there, and its leathery point softly plows the mud as it is driven back and forth. Jak-Ur keeps pounding.

I sneak up to Jak-Ur from behind, silent and light-footed like a kitten. I am only six feet away, and I hear a moan, was it a squealing, a wailing, *my brother, you are not dead yet*, Jak-Ur rides him like dogs ride bitches, and I have no fear anymore, my soul explodes, I summon all the rage in my head, and the bursting of my heart and I make it into strength for my legs and I run, and with my whole body give Jak-Ur's back one push.

The stone wall has rotted, the mud between the stones is soft from the autumn rains, and Jak-Ur's weight pushes brother down, and brother's weight pulls Jak-Ur down. Jak-Ur startled tries to turn around, to grab something, but he can't stop the fall, brother is still alive and holds to the savage's one leg that still stands on the ground and brother pulls the leg down with him, and they are both gone in the dark hole, it is only a breath, two breaths, the well is thirty feet deep, not more, and I hear a dull thud. Both as one. And then I hear Jak-Ur scream as if he broke something. Now, after six days, I know that he hobbles badly; he can only stand on one leg. I don't hear brother screaming; I don't hear him wailing anymore.

"Do not be afraid, little brother. I saved you. A peaceful death to end your shame. And I'll avenge you. Not just Jak-Ur. I'll fill wells like this one with the blood of these monsters. I will."

My name is Sarah.

Watch me.

III.

Your Own Heart

Thirteenth Winter. The Sieve. First Day.

Red was the second color of the day. The maulers stopped tearing Ughi's thighs, and the small open carcass was left to fill up with red water. It caught the rain, falling heavier now, like a warped cauldron, a cup for the Reekaal.

Not much later, the riders emerged as wind spirits born out of the hazy dawn. Three hooded shadows on horseback stopped in front of us. One of them had a female frame: a black robe split in the middle and the sides. Her legs straddled the horse snugly. She dismounted and walked toward us, the two Guides on either side.

"Sah-Ouna," whispered Elbia. Her voice, sweet as a nightingale's song, turned my fear into a mythical adventure.

"Sah-Ouna, the First Ouna-Ma," said Atares. Sah-Ouna slowly raised her arrow finger. Silence.

I was at the end of the line, and she came to me first. Her skin pale, her eyebrows dark serpents. She sank her nails into my cheeks and turned my head to the right to look at the back of my neck. The fingers of her other hand, icy cold worms, slithered through my hair searching for something. From that night, she would be the one Demon who would haunt and hunt me.

"Worthy…to face the three deaths," Sah-Ouna whispered to me. She mimed spitting on me but then moved to Atares.

"Worthy to face the three deaths."

The third one was Elbia.

"Worthy to face all deaths."

And so it went. Each kid, one by one, until she reached a boy who was coughing badly and couldn't even raise his eyes to look at her. She passed him without saying the words or spitting. A Guide grabbed the boy, and they disappeared into the darkness.

"He is finished," I heard Atares.

A whistling sound cut through the rain. An arrow landed between Atares's legs, and he froze in place. Murky Eyes approached fast on foot.

"No talking and no moving, rats."

The tall Archer boy standing next to Ughi's torn body warmed the mud as his piss ran down his shaky knees. He had kept his stare down since the maulers left. Shaky Knees would be next.

I could see hardly anything around me. The rain was falling again like a veil of crystal thorns. I didn't want to see. Nothing else. No one. I closed my eyes so as not to meet those of any other child. They stole my strength every time they looked at me. The darkness and the medley of sounds soon made me dizzy, and I opened my eyes again.

Before the pale sun was at mid-horizon, Shaky Knees finally fell, mumbling, "No, no." When he hit the mud, no arrow struck him, no Guide cut his throat, and no mauler came to tear him to pieces.

Others soon followed. I counted the children around me, fewer than three times the fingers on my one hand remained standing. My knees started shaking. The day before, I had carried the pails till dusk without rest. The cold was twisting blades in my back. Almost defeated. But she saved me. The mud. Brown and wet like the pulp of horseshit and piss I had been drenched in since my seventh winter. I could see the Greentooth's reflection, the one who sent me out every day at dawn in the dreadful heat and bitter cold, there. She was looking up at me, cursing me, ugly, but for once useful. "You? At the Sieve? Huh! You'll fall on the first day. They'll send you back here to the shit pails."

She was right; they wouldn't kill all of us. But if I fell, I would be thrown back into the world of that pulp from which there was no return. Its stink penetrated everything forever. Faced with it there was neither hot nor cold, nor any pain in the knees. I closed my eyes and saw the warrior on his gray-white horse that kicked over my pail. How strong and fearsome he looked. My legs turned iron hard.

Each of our warriors had three horses. And there were more warriors than anyone could ever count. And there was something more I knew: "How much does a horse crap in a day?"

I didn't know the bow, but I knew that.

"About my weight in shit every day."

I could pass into old age, many rainless summers, carrying steaming pails mixed with my own sweat and golden-green flies. And still, I wouldn't have carried in one long life even what the whole of Sirol shat out in three days.

As I stood there looking at the thick brown mud around my feet, I said to myself and to the Greentooth that I wasn't going back to the shit even if they kept us standing for one moon. The Greentooth was not my mother. Every night, I wished for the heads of Darhul to come out and take her before the next day dawned. But she taught me more than my real mother ever could have. Others would fall. I would not.

There were a couple of girls among those still standing. I moved between Elbia and Atares. I was not going to fall in front of her feet. She reached over to me with her fist and touched me. A smile, not a smirk. "Hold on. Don't fall. It's almost over."

Her hand was covered in mud. It was warm and soft, like life.

"What's over?" I asked. Before I finished my words, a reed arrow landed three fingers from my foot.

The Guides threw into carts the children who fell. Unconscious or dead, I knew not. When each cart filled with four or five, the Guides took them away. But it would end.

It was early evening, and eight of us were still standing. Elbia, Atares, and Urak from the Blades, another girl, two boys I didn't know, and Malan. They had brought him into the orphans just one winter ago, after our warriors' raids in the South. His skin was milky white, but they told us that he was one of us and not an othertriber.

Finally, one of the nameless boys fell. The second horseman dismounted and took off his hood. He was a Reghen, a Truthsayer, his gray robe marked by the red circle. His voice was as strong as ten warriors' as he spoke. My whole life gushed out of his chest:

The Truth of the Sieve

Children of the Archers, the Rods, and the Blades, the Hunters, and the Craftsmen, the Trackers, the Tanners, and the orphans: Prick up your ears like the Wolf, plant your legs like the stallion, and hear now the Truth of the Tribe's Sieve.

The twelfth winter is upon you, and the Sieve will decree where the next one will find you.

This first night, the Wolfmen, the protectors, and the Guides of the Tribe came and gathered you from your tents, which you will never see again.

Into trials of the Sieve you will enter for a moon and a half and the eyes of Enaka, the One Goddess of the Unending Sky, will be upon you.

Only the strong will leave the Sieve as warriors. Hunger and ice will become your brother and your sister. Dung and rotten fish are the fate of the weak. The Wolfmen, your Guides, will allow no sheep-heart to waste a warrior's bow. Guides you will call the old warriors, who in winter will place you on the path of the true Golden Sun and Silver Selene.

Enaka watches from above, and from her lips the winds of victory blow upon you. Become Warriors. Stand by her in the Final Battle. Do not end up in the nine jaws of Darhul.

As sheep for slaughter, you enter the Sieve,
as ashen wolves of the steppe, you will leave.

Thus declared the Ouna-Mas, the Voices of the Unending Sky.

For countless nights, each breath and word unchanged, I heard the Truth of the Sieve. That was the only thing any boy my age wanted to talk about. Old Man left a basket between ours and the Reghen's feet. The smell of meat.

"Seven pieces. One for each. You are the Wolves of the first night. No meat for those who fell, the Sheep. That's it for today," the Reghen shouted. The gray-hooded man looked young from up close, only a few winters older than me.

I wanted to let out a cry of joy, but nothing came. I wanted to run, but I was too tired and numb from the cold, so my legs shuffled to the basket. Urak got there first and grabbed three pieces of meat, but Atares and another boy fell on him, kicking and punching until he was left bruised and stunned. Atares took the last and smallest piece of meat and dipped it in the mud before shoving it into Urak's mouth. Danaka, the second girl, cheered him on. So did I.

"Go over there to eat," said Old Man, pointing to the only tent at the southwest corner of the field. I stole a glance to the left of me and saw other Guides dragging the last cart of the day to the tents on the opposite side with a few children in them.

"Will we see them again?" I asked.

Elbia looked at me with puzzled brown eyes. Beautiful.

"The Sheep? Why, yes. Hasn't your mother taught you anything?"

"What mother? He's an orphan," said Atares.

"Worthless orphans. Two of them are still standing today. I can't believe it," said the other boy, whose name I didn't know.

Murky Eyes came next to me as we were talking. He lifted my mane and looked at the back of my neck as Sah-Ouna had done earlier. His stinking mouth was gaping and silent. I was staring at the slots under his eyebrows. His eyes were covered with gray-white clouds.

"The Reekaal got him," Atares whispered. Murky Eyes lifted his hand and slapped the babbling boy.

The Tribe had many Legends because we had too many demons to fight. The most horrifying of all were the Reekaal, the bloodeaters of the

Forest. No one had ever been able to describe them in detail. Whoever had seen them lost forever the life and the black from their eyes. They turned to a cloudy gray, and most times so did their minds. Just like the man standing in front of me.

The same Legend said that the only way to kill a Reekal was to offer him your own heart. No one dared lie about ever killing a Reekaal. But the Greentooth who raised us repeated the Legend so many times that it had become engraved inside me. They were senseless words, but I couldn't forget them.

"The Demon always looks you in the eye. And she knows all she needs."

She? The Demon is a She?

The Greentooth continued.

"Never in the heart. She cannot bear that. If you want to defeat the Demon, you must rip out your own heart and offer it to her. Then she will fall on her knees and sing her grieving song to you. And that will be her end and yours as you both sink to the bottom of the Blackvein River, together, in the last embrace."

But who could ever rip out his own heart? It took me seven lives and deaths to learn that.

Wolf

Apocrypha II.
I Want to Be Your Goddess

Now, you are down there, and I am up here. I have the power and the bucket, and you are the one begging. I want you to beg me, not to curse me, that's why I didn't even approach the well the first two days. I didn't want you to think that I was the one who pushed you. For you, I am going to be the one who keeps you alive. I am going to be water, bread, hope, your only chance that you will not sleep your last sleep curled around the skeleton of my brother. No matter what wretched bitch spat you out, no matter your savagery, this is a punishment even you can be scared of.

I have a torch. I have tar, cloth, fire, oil, and wood, and I can set it ablaze anytime and see your face down there. I don't need the sun or the moon. But I want you to pray for the sky's lights; I want to be your goddess, the one who rides the moon chariot and tames the sun rays, the one who comes only when you pray hard.

I have an ox. I keep it far away by the chicken barn so that you never hear it bellow. Otherwise, you'd know that I could harness it to pull you out of there. You wonder where your horse is.

I had a dog. Kinos the White. A hound from the Thousand Islands, a restless thing, the color of curdled milk, not quite white, that I had since he was a puppy. I was seven then, and he was old now. Back then I was afraid of him. He wanted to play and never stood still, as hunting dogs do, but I was too little to know that. I spent days and nights terrified of that puppy that I later came to love more than anything. My father mocked my fear, then had me be the one who fed him the scraps and bring him water. I would tremble as little Kinos jumped on me every evening, impatient and joyful. But father was right. Soon I became the master, the one who brings the water and the food. I had a puppy once. I trained it well. It would wag its tail and stare at me with bright eyes. Just like you are going to do.

I want you to dream of Sarah all day, with your eyes wide open.

So now, you think, you hope, that I was not the one who pushed you down the well. Hope and fear mold the truths.

That chubby priest helped with that; God help him now.

He came alone on the third day on a mule, he had heard of raids farther north—he'd never have come if he knew that the infidels had reached our village. He came to warn us he said, but I think he wanted to secure his trophy before it was too late. I hid so that he wouldn't find me until a thought crossed my mind. He turned around to leave when he saw the corpses scattered around the huts, but I ran and stopped him.

"Help me, father."

"What...what?" He didn't seem happy to see me.

He was mumbling, trying to grasp what had happened here. Jak-Ur started screaming as if he'd heard the priest. He couldn't have heard his mumbles, probably smelled his stench. My mother said that the priest never washed unless it was a great holy day. It was her only effort to console me. Fortunately, there are five of these each year, holy days that is.

"A barbarian," I say, a smirk on my face contrasting the priest's sweating agony. He doesn't answer, he shivers.

"Oh don't worry, it is thirty feet deep. He can't come out."

The priest walks with arms and legs wide, favoring one leg to balance his weight. Priests of the Faith are allowed to marry. God demands that they have many children, even girls, and they always choose wives much younger than them to endure the pregnancies. Nine is an evil number; a good wife should strive for twelve as the number of the months of our Savior and the sacred elders of the books. Swollen bellies for girls with hardly any fuzz between their legs, swollen bellies until our hair turns white.

The priest approaches the stone rim of the well, with furtive steps. It is noon, and the light is bright as he looks down. Jak-Ur screams. The priest is the very first face Jak-Ur sees. The one he'll hate. The priest doesn't give water or food to Jak-Ur, he mumbles more holy words and then steps back and disappears from Jak-Ur's view.

"We must bury the dead," the priest says.

We, means I have to do it, he is not one to dig ten graves. I'm not either, even if I had the strength and the will I wouldn't. I didn't kill any of them. I buried Kinos.

"We will return with more men to make it right. It's time to go." *I take you with me to give me twelve children. Boys to serve God, the Emperor, or become slaves to the barbarians.* "Did you?" The priest dares to ask me finally.

"Me, no! How could I? It was my brother who pulled him down there. He is still there."

"Who?"

"My brother. He is still down there with him."

The priest covers his nose with the back of his hand. Only now does he realize what the reek that wafts up from the well is.

"We must come back to bury them. Anastasis," he says.

"Can't we just burn them?" I ask, my brow creasing playfully.

"Anastasis," he repeats with a stronger voice, to erase my blasphemy.

Anastasis. Again, to stand.

Resurrection.

I know the words of the faith, it is just that I don't understand them. The dead have to be buried to rise from their bones; they can't rise from ashes. This God of ours seems weak or one of peculiar habits. Why does he need the bones of all things? Is he going to glue them back together one by one, slather them with fresh flesh? Is he going to use them as rolling pins, flesh for flour, to smoothen out the new muscle? Butter for fat? And then wrap it all together, like the cheese, honey, and walnut pies Mother used to make. She would have made one today; it is the Seventh Day of the Moon. And then? Will God kneel down and blow young dreams down the ears of the risen or will he leave all the sadness inside? Does he work so carefully with each cadaver, as the carpenter works the wood? Why can't he just speak an incantation and make the dead rise again?

"Can you walk?" the priest asks. I see his lips moving; his brimmed hat covers his eyes completely.

He needs the mule; I am the one who must walk. It may be his weight that forces him to ask, but probably not.

"Yes, I can. But, let me show you something first, father. Come to the barn. Give me your hat."

How could I ever marry one whom I must call "father?"

It is the eighth day now that Jak-Ur is trapped down there. The fifth after the priest came. I showed my face for the first time to Jak-Ur, that same night after he saw the priest. That was the first time I brought him water and bread. We started to make signs. I gestured a fat man pushing him down the well. He gestured for a rope to pull him up. A ladder. His horse. But the horse ran away moments after Jak-Ur fell. A rope. Yes. There used to be a bucket tied to a beam, a pulley, and a lever. When I was a kid and the well's water was still cold and pure we'd put a watermelon in the bucket and lower it. Cold watermelons. I devoured them, but my brother never liked them, as if he knew. But even if I had the bucket and the pulley they wouldn't hold the weight of Jak-Ur. *I am here for you. I'll pull you out with my bare hands.* I scream, I pull, I grunt, Jak-Ur tries to press his boots onto the wall. One step, up, two steps, he climbs. Those stones are slippery, very slippery.

I have oil; I said that. Sometimes at night, I come and slowly drip it down the wall, without him seeing me. I must make sure he never makes it alone. I can't pull him out either; I don't have the strength. He climbs six feet up the wall and then falls down again, bellows in anger, looks at me in despair. I step back. I wait a few moments. He shouts. I return.

Don't you worry, pig. I am not going to leave you. I haven't killed you yet.

I've thought of thirteen deaths.

One: I stop giving him water.

Two: I give him water but no food.

Three: I throw stones at him. The priest would do that. Like God did to the infidels, but I don't want to throw anything; what if he finds a way to use these stones and climb? I don't like this death. It is weak. Makes me weak.

Four: I go hunt in the forest. Not there, close to the pile of corpses, where the scavengers come at night. Capture a jackal, a wildcat, an adder. Capture them and throw them all down the well. Alive. Can't capture such beasts easily.

Five: Hay and fire, the screams. Purification; end this reek forever. But I saw Ion the Hunter, my father's friend, burn in the flaming arrows of the archers a few days ago. He screamed, but it all ended so fast. No.

Six: Do nothing. How long can he stand with my brother's corpse there? How many nights can he lean on the walls to sleep next to the worms that forget who is dead and who is just asleep?

Seven: Keep feeding him and never let him out. A man dies if his legs rot. One of his legs is hurt, and there is no room to sleep or walk. That alone will kill him sooner or later.

Eight: The snow and the cold. The winter will be harsh. The freezing rain will start soon. He is lightly clad. A leather jerkin, trousers, and boots but bare arms, he won't last long. I can let him freeze to death. An almost peaceful death. No.

Nine: I go to the priest's town, and ask for the men to come with me and kill him. I hope they can do as much.

Ten: The bones of the dead. Throw down the corpses of all they murdered, my nana, my father, the charred body of Ion, One-Eyed

Palas, the old warrior who came with my father—he had served under him—the woodcutter's girls. The girls would always come for broth when we slaughtered a chicken. I had to pluck the birds, alive and jerking headless after I put them in the boiled water, but the girls would never come to help me when I plucked. Only when the broth was ready. I count fifteen corpses fast. Maybe more. One by one, throw them down there, bury him in the dead.

I am counting past ten now; it helps that I am barefoot.

Eleven: A wasp hive.

Twelve: Pretend to pull him up then throw him down again. It is a scary one, but it can be done. The ox pulls him up; he is almost there. He can smell fresh air again. The despair in his voice, the hope, that one moment. And then I cut the rope and he falls again. I like that.

Thirteen: The one I haven't thought of yet. I am sure there are more ways to kill Jak-Ur. I'll leave him there until I think of a better death.

He shouldn't have touched my brother.

I had a brother once. He was still alive when I pushed Jak-Ur. Did I kill my brother?

I had a dog once. His name was Kinos. The color of curdled milk, until the molossus grabbed his leg. Still, Kinos didn't die; he was still alive when they went down the well. I had to, with an ax.

I have an ox.

I have an ax.

I tie the ax to the rope, and I lower it.

It is time to get my brother out.

IV.
Roast Meat

Thirteenth Winter. The Sieve. Second Night.

Ughi. The maulers. They were all sleeping silent. I buried my teeth into the horse meat. It was a thick piece, roasted over a real fire, not a thin slice dried in the sun. I was tearing it apart.

We were sitting in a large round tent. Poles pounded into the dirt formed a circle about our height. They were covered with horse hides and sheep skins. A second row of thinner poles tied on top of them bent toward the center, making the roof. The skins were heavy and fresh, not like the torn ones that let the wind and rain through. I saw a stack of hides, waist-long woolen tunics, leather trousers, felt stockings, and horsehair boots. We punched and kicked for the best boots until we each got a pair. They were all the same, and there were plenty for all of us. I dressed and sat next to the fire to feel my hands and feet again.

Urak's groans, and the blood running from his nose, made a good background for our feast. The Guides who had snatched us were in the tent watching. They had taken off their wolf hats and finally looked like old men. Wings had lifted my heart, and I was enjoying the spoils. At death's first call, I had come out alive and a winner. And with a belly full of meat. It was the most beautiful night of my life, the night that I was born again.

My neck bent heavy as a log, and my eyes kept shutting. Yet sleep was long in coming. I wanted to talk. And to listen. "You are the Wolves tonight, but come morning, you will all wish you'd slept," said Murky Eyes.

"No one sleeps the first night. Let them be," said Old Man as they stepped out of the tent, leaving us alone for the first time.

There were spare skins scattered around the fire and room for more children to sleep. *More children, where were they?* The two girls were still eating and no one cared to speak before the last morsel of meat.

"This was roast meat, cooked with fire," was the first thing I said.

"What did you expect? Rat?" asked the only one of the seven whose name I still didn't know.

I didn't understand. I had eaten rat once during the Great Feast of Spring.

"Rat?" Dried under the saddle. The horse's salty sweat softening the meat. "Once," I answered.

The boy spat with disgust in the dirt between us. The Sky, the Witch, and now this boy were spitting mercilessly on me. Even though I was a winner.

"I am Bako of the Archers, and I eat horsemeat all the time," said the boy. His neck was jutting out of his shoulders as if he were announcing something of great importance to the whole Tribe. And that's how I learned the last one's name.

"They say that the end of the first night of the Sieve is half a warrior's training," said Danaka across from me.

She cared not for rats or orphans. She had strong legs but the voice of a girl half her age. And nothing else that I would ever notice again. My gaze returned to Elbia even before Danaka finished her words.

"Why do you tell him lies? A warrior's training lasts five times spring," said Atares.

"What half training? We're still in the Sieve to see what banner we will be sent to. Then we begin training. I will become an Archer, and that orphan, if he doesn't die here first, will be making my boots," answered Bako.

"You are not an Archer yet. You come from the tents where the young of the Archers are raised."

"Same thing."

"You don't know anything," said Elbia.

Every time Elbia spoke, the fire in front of me swelled and brightened. My shoulders straightened so that I wouldn't slouch, and my eyes opened wide. I wiped my lips with the back of my hand to get rid of the last bit of meat, drool and dried mud stuck around my mouth.

"Tell me."

She turned to face only me and said: "Yes, it is true what he says. Training lasts five times spring. But those who know say that the first day, today, is the hardest, as hard as half the five winters' training."

"If we survive the one-and-a-half-moon trial of the Sieve," Bako said again.

"A few winters back, the Sieve lasted one moon, but once it took almost two moons," Elbia said.

"Yes, one moon; that was the black winter when the northfrost came early," said Atares, staring at the weak fire.

I didn't know much about the Sieve, but I knew that in a field of snow and ice none of us would stand a chance. Naked and barefoot.

Urak was sleeping off his beating. Every time he snored, Atares would get up and kick him in the ass to make him stop. Malan was the only one who didn't talk at all. He had his arms crossed on top of his knees and was staring at the mud. He was an orphan too.

On one side of the tent was a stack of pots, some big and some small, and on the other were strewn a couple of poles and cudgels, and a whip. No blades or bows. I let out a sigh of relief. Almost everyone in the tent was better than I with the weapons. If we were to compete with bows the next day, I wouldn't be among the winners, the Wolves.

"It's going to be like that every day," Atares said. "Guides, Reghen, Ouna-Mas. Sieving. They'll keep coming."

"And the Wolfmen. Those I fear most," Danaka whispered.

"That is only Legend," Atares replied.

"No, it isn't. They come in the Sieve, always, with the first snow."

My head and my mind were whirling from one mouth to the other to keep up.

"What Wolfmen?" I asked.

Bako motioned with one hand to the girls to stop. He knew.

"It is no Legend. We might be called Wolves, but we are not real Wolfmen."

"What's a real one like?"

"Wolf's head, hide, tail, two legs. Teeth."

"That's a tale."

"No, the Ouna-Mas lie with those men, the Guides, when Selene is full and turn them into Wolfmen. They then send them to purge the Sieve. The Reghen talked of Wolfmen in his Truths. He said it, don't you remember?"

Danaka nodded yes.

"These are tales. For children," Atares insisted.

"No, the Wolfmen will come. They are the ones who bring white death. You will see. Before the end of the Sieve."

Atares turned to me.

"You listen to me, Da-Ren. Forget about him. The Ouna-Mas don't waste their time with the old Guides; won't even talk to them. The Ouna-Mas mate only with the Khun and the Chiefs."

"Even when the Ouna-Mas ride the warriors, they never speak to them," Bako blurted out.

"What do you mean *they ride them*?" asked Danaka.

"You haven't bled yet, huh? Don't worry, they won't be riding you anyway."

Elbia was looking at me. Again. I raised my shoulders straight.

"Hey, you, wake up," Bako shouted to Malan. He had yet to speak a word. "You, stupid orphan. Have you seen a girl bleeding?"

Malan just ignored him, so Bako turned his attention to me.

"Have you?"

I mumbled "Yes," but Bako didn't believe me. He kept on talking.

"Not like that other orphan, who bled first today. Those maulers. It was fast. Haven't they taught you anything? What did you do all day?"

"Every day…we carried. Fresh horse piss for the hides and horseshit to dry for the fires. Sometimes—"

"Ha! Horse piss for the hides, he says. Why they'd bring you here?

Your pal was smart. He got away from the first night. No more pain."

Bako got up and mimicked Ughi shaking at the knees and falling. Then, with his palm held flat in front of his neck, he made the motion of the Guide's blade when it slit Ughi's throat. Bako bleated mockingly, then laughed.

I was on my two feet and ready to pounce on him, when Atares held me back. It was too late.

"You wanna fight, horseshit? Come on, grab one. Blade fight."

I had fallen into his trap. Bako got up, threw me one of the two wooden poles lying next to him and stood ready across from me, holding his pole like a sword. The pole already reached the tent's ceiling where it was lower along the sides. This was no place for a blade fight. There was no room to run, no way for my legs to save me.

"Block his blade, Da-Ren. Hold high. Two hands," Elbia got up and cheered me on.

I grabbed the pole with two hands like a heavy sword and got up to face him. All this fuss woke even Urak. Everyone made for the sides of the tent to give us room. My legs were shaking as in the field.

I knew what I was up against. Every day I roamed most of the camp to find the fresh piss. I had seen the eleven-wintered Archer children, strong and proud, parrying and thrusting the wooden poles, again and again. They weren't carrying pails of shit. I had no luck.

I countered his strikes four times, but I didn't have the skill. On the fifth strike, Bako's pole hit my wrist hard and the pain blinded me. On the sixth, the pole fell from my hands and lay, defeated, in the fire. Bako pointed to the hides.

"Kneel and say, 'I am a horseshit orphan.'"

I didn't move. Not even my eyes moved. I didn't want to catch Elbia's stare.

He lifted his pole to hit me. I closed my eyes and raised my arms to cover my head. I opened them two breaths later to see Malan between Bako and me. Malan had grabbed the pole with both hands and Bako was trying to free it.

"You cannot, you stupid orphan. No hands on blade," Bako shouted to Malan, still trying unsuccessfully to free his pole.

"What blade?" were Malan's first words that night as he secured Bako's wooden pole in his fists. In the time it took Bako to think of all the rules of proper training, Malan kneed him in the balls.

Bako fell on his back, writhing in pain. "In practice. No, you can't, no hands on blade," he was still mumbling, holding his crotch with both hands.

"Practice?" asked Malan with a grin, as he fell onto Bako's chest and wrapped his knees around him. He landed two punches in Bako's nose—it broke on the first—and then pushed his bloodied face three fingers from the fire.

"Roast meat, Da-Ren. Cooked on fire. Want some? Orphans don't get that," Malan said in a low steady voice, his head turning toward me.

The red-hot dung coals were already touching Bako's cheek. Screaming and bleeding. The Guides rushed through the hides. If they were a couple of breaths slower, Bako would have been marked forever. The whip hit the fire, sending embers flying everywhere. We all fell down and played dead.

The Guides stayed until we shut up for good. Silence fell, and broke only by the crackling of the fire and the dogs' barking, not too far off.

Malan lay down next to me, and Bako crawled away from us. He wouldn't sleep next to the fire. He was Bako, from the tents where the young of the brave Archers were reared, where they were taught how to blade fight with wooden poles. In practice. Once the Guides left and the dogs quieted down, he bade me goodnight.

"You will bleed tomorrow, shit carriers. I spit on the slave bitches who gave birth to you. They spat you out and died in pain, when they saw your shit faces. You have no warrior blood in you," Bako continued to mumble. He couldn't sleep either.

"No orphan piss boy makes it through the Sieve alive," I heard Danaka saying.

"Shut up and sleep," Elbia whispered back at her.

I would sleep the night next to her.

"It's true. They bring them here to have meat for the dogs. You'll see tomorrow when they fall first."

The warmth of the fire and the girls' sweet whispering melted my turmoil, and my eyelids finally closed. Only for a little while.

V.
I Dreamed of Cauldrons

Thirteenth Winter. The Sieve. Second Night.

I dreamed of cauldrons.

Fat entrails and bloody guts were bubbling in there, and Ughi was stirring, holding a pole with his two hands. Blood was slowly dripping into the pot from his open neck. He brought his arrow finger to his lips, motioning me not to make a sound.

The sounds woke me, many and loud, as a man's shouting orders ended everyone's sleep.

"On your feet."

The side of my face close to the fire was burning like the coals. My feet, away from it, were ice cold. I was slowly getting up when Old Man pushed me. "Quickly, move next to them."

I protected my head, afraid that someone would start pulling me out of the tent like the night before. It was still black outside, not a single ray of light seeping through the hides. I squatted next to the other children.

The Reghen, the gray-clad youth who had thrown us the meat, was passing out a thick milk and millet gruel. We ate his warm gift straight out of our cupped hands. Soon, the new day would dawn and it would bring another trial. No Reghen had ever come to my tent to speak. I was never sent to their camp to load pails, so I had made up a few tales of my own that they were all creatures born of fire and iron and they didn't shit or piss.

I remembered Elbia's words. *The first day is half the training.*

It was.

It was the moment of the first awakening. The Wolves' tent with the fresh-skinned hides, the voices of the Guides that replaced the Greentooth's, the voice of Elbia yesterday, and her apple-red cheeks now, me licking the Reghen's gruel from my fingers, all of this meant that I was an orphan no more.

Would I become a warrior? Would I end up as meat for the dogs? Only the stars knew that. But already I was a Wolf not an orphan. Even if I ran in the mud and the snow with horses, bows, and blades for five springs until my eighteenth winter when I would be a worthy warrior, it would still be only the other half of my training.

The Reghen was not alone. With him was the red-veiled Ouna-Ma and the same two Guides from the previous night. Atares turned to me as if I were his dumb little orphan child and said, "The Reghen is going to tell us a Story."

"No, he is going to tell us a Truth," said Elbia.

The Reghen turned his back on us and fell to one knee in front of the Ouna-Ma. Her fingers, painted with black henna ornaments all the way to the elbow, emerged from her black robe and pressed on the Reghen's forehead. I could see nothing of her face. A thick red veil was wrapped around her head except for a small gap around the eyes. The man and woman stood still and exchanged wild, unintelligible whispers. After a while, the Ouna-Ma disappeared deep into the shadows of the tent. The Reghen rose, took off his hood, turned to us, and spoke:

The Truth of the First Night

We are commanded by the Sun of Enaka, the voice of the Ouna-Ma, and the bow of Khun-Taa, Fifth Leader of the Tribe. And we listen.

The trial of the Sieve will persist every day until Enaka's glorious warriors of tomorrow stand apart from those lesser in strength, the weaklings that will carry no blade or bow, and, even worse, from the wretched cowards. Those, the Sieve will keep forever.

Neither bow, nor horse, nor blades shall the twelve-wintered of the Sieve see in the trials.

Three deaths will the children of the Sieve face:

Cold.

Hunger.

And the third, the unspeakable, the terrible.

What fate is deserved by each and every one of you will be decreed by Enaka, and she will tell only the First, Sah-Ouna, who will pass this wisdom down to the Ouna-Mas and the Reghen.

The First Reghen have forged the Truths of the Sieve, five generations past.

Listen to them now:

On the first day, the first who falls will twice be put to death, once with an iron blade and once with the blade of a beast.

This first, weakest of souls is the poison of Darhul and must not live among us. Do not spit at the feeble-bodied in the face, but send them to the tents of the help to live as Fishermen, Blacksmiths, and Tanners. But rip out the soul of the faint-hearted, the first one to fall, and only him, and into the Great River, the Blackvein, throw him unburned, before his poison spreads to the rest.

This is the Story that you will bring to the victors' tent, the Wolves, on the second night before they go out again. In the weaklings' tents, the Sheep, only horse dung and tar. May no Reghen or Ouna-Ma ever set foot there.

Thus declared the Ouna-Mas, the Voices of The Unending Sky.

The Reghen and the Ouna-Ma turned their backs on us and left without another word. Ughi, the poison of the Tribe, traveled unburned in the Blackvein, and I would never dream of him again.

They took us outside. No raindrop glimmered in the moonlight, and that made the darkness deeper than the first night even.

Old Man took me out of my thoughts. "Throw hides and boots in the first shed, leave only the loincloth on, and stand in line."

"Again, the same?" I asked the others.

Atares shrugged his shoulders. He didn't know either.

"So, the Ouna-Ma doesn't go to the Sheep's tents?" Bako asked Murky Eyes. The Guide slapped him hard and then answered, "Today, when you fall, you will see."

Bako didn't know everything after all.

"To those who fell? No, the Reghen and the Ouna-Ma will never go to them. But they were not hurt. There they are."

Elbia pointed to the moving torches on the right. Guides and a herd of children were approaching the field.

"And how do they learn?" I asked.

"You will tell them. So the weak come to respect the strong," Old Man answered.

"But they live," said Elbia.

"Yes, they are called Sheep, but if they slaughter us all like sheep... Who will become warrior?" said Atares.

"So, the maulers won't tear apart the first to fall today?" asked Danaka.

"No."

"Are you sure?"

"I think so."

Apocrypha III.
A Thousand Sickles Fell on Them

As the One Mother heard the Legends, Chapter III

I dreamt of fields covered with dead frogs.

"Kill a frog, kill your mother," said the witch.

How many times has my mother died by now?

I am not afraid of the witch. She started coming to the settlement after the fifteenth night. She never gets very close; she stays where the parsnip field ends, and the forest begins. She watches me, slender and swaying in the wind like the beech trees. She is the only living being that has come so close since the priest.

It is important for a small hamlet like ours to have its witch. I remember once I broke the milk jar coming back from the cow barn. I was twelve back then, and I didn't say anything to anyone. I left the pieces close to the beech wood all night. In the morning when my mother asked for it, I swore that I had brought it back in. They found the broken jar under the same tree where the witch stands tonight. They all blamed the witch.

Once, the woodcutter's wife set fire to their longhouse by mistake. I saw her run out, with the baby—not all my stories are sad—but there was no one else around. She told me that she had left the haystack and the baby close to the hearth, and made me promise to the twelve saints that I wouldn't tell anyone, else her man would beat her to death. She blamed the witch. They believed her.

The witch's baby did not survive. They said it perished of fever in the forest hut, soon after my father exiled both of them from our land. Berries and parsnips are no food for a baby. It was after that she'd appear on the coldest nights, open a door and show her face, scream, curse, throw stones at the sheep and disappear. Still, I am not afraid of her; neither was Kinos. I had a puppy once.

I remember when I was twelve I stole a pear and disappeared by the southern barn to eat it. My father was there, with the witch, a year before she became a witch. I look a lot like her, I know that, though no one ever dared to say it. He had embraced her, and they were both swaying as Jak-Ur and my little brother were swaying forty days ago. In the end, my father moaned then laughed a roaring laughter and slapped her bare bottom once, before he pushed her away. Father wasn't afraid of her. Why should I be?

Her belly started growing after that, and the priest came and said that it was the work of the Devil. Everybody believed him, except for my mother I think. I remember her spitting on the mud, and leaving the big house hearth while all the men were still arguing. They let us young stay through the whole argument. What kind of witch she was, that was the question. Was she a *vrlak*, one who wakes at midnight to feed on the living? No one had seen her do that. Was she just a false healer, one who reads the fortunes and tends the sick? Yes, they had seen her try to help the cattle with the blue-green dust, and she'd always look at men as if she knew what they were going to do. They always want to do the same thing. "Yes, a healer," they agreed, and she was exiled to certain death in the dark woodland. The pack of wolves has grown bigger in there; the Hunter never finds a deer alive anymore.

But why should I be afraid of a healer?

The witch comes now and observes me and the well at night. She doesn't come closer; she doesn't scream or throw stones anymore. The serfs and the old warriors had made up tales: *She doesn't have any toes, she washes in pig's blood, she turns the parsnips green and the turnips red, she devoured her baby.*

Now that I am a bit older I can put the truths together. That baby of hers was my half-brother. I used to have two brothers.

It is important for a small hamlet like ours to have its witch. Else we would have murdered each other a long time before the barbarians came.

The rag doll I am afraid of. I dreamt of her. I hope it was a dream. Nana gave me the rag doll back when I was young and dreamt only of honey and warm bread. And Crispus, the boy with the curly hair. I used to dream of him a lot.

Nana sewed her out of sackcloth and fattened her with hay, back when she could trust her hands and eyes for such work. It was a scary faceless thing. I had to paint the doll's eyes and mouth with chicken blood, paint some life on her sackcloth cheeks. It was the only one I had, so her only name was *rag doll*. She had black goat-hair glued to her head, and not much of a nose. I look a lot like her, I know that, though no one ever dared to say it. She was about the size of my forearm, and she disappeared the evening that the priest came.

The ax was no good. Jak-Ur had no space to wield it. I gave him a sickle; I didn't want to throw my good knife at him. A sickle is even worse, but I have to make him suffer somehow. He knows I can't lift a whole body. He has to chop it up to eight pieces or more, fill the burlap sack eight times. One load was only dead leaves and crawling mud. He has been going on all day, chopping and digging with rage, to get rid of my brother. He keeps digging like that, and he'll soon reach the hell where he belongs.

I don't care what the priest said; I am not going to bury them. If all the dead build their new houses here, then the living have to run away. Not my brother or my nana.

I took the sheep out of the fold and brought those animals to the longhouse where I sleep. They are on one side now, and I am on the other. Winter is here; both they and I need the warmth. The manure separates their space and mine. The sheepfold I turned into a grave for all the dead. Or a bed for a pyre, I should say. I have gathered all the dead there, and all that came out of the sacks. Nana is there. If it were not for that drizzling rain, I would have finished by now. I gathered faggots, and I have oil and tar.

I thought that Jak-Ur would be in peace now that he is all alone. Yet he seems worse. Maybe it is the cold, maybe that he now has space to rest and accept his fate. He seems dejected, his back against the stone wall, his eyes always looking down to nothing. He doesn't lift his gaze when

I appear and shout at him. He will die there like that; sad and peaceful. I don't want that. He will die believing that I was the one who tried to save him, wrapped in a shroud of kindness and hope. No, that can't happen.

Maybe it is my fault; I wanted to become his Goddess. By now he is convinced. It was that day after he chopped up my brother's body. I then lowered a bucket of water. Then some spelt bread and even some roasted gosling. Only time I gave him meat; I was celebrating too, it was time to get brother out of there. Now that my brother is gone, I approach the well and there is no fear, only hatred.

I then lowered the bucket a third time. The priest's head was in it; green like a fresh watermelon. Kill a frog...

"See, I killed him for you. Cut his throat with the sickle. I cut the one who threw you down there."

And you understand what I am saying. We all speak the one tongue of blood.

Jak-Ur lifted the severed head by its scant oily hair and bellowed in joy. It didn't last long, joy never does. I didn't give him any meat after that. The last few days I gave him only parsnips and turnips. Parsnips green as the frog, turnips red as the priest. Watermelons.

The settlement is not something that one woman, even a young one like me, can keep going. It might be only a few plethra of land, but still one has to plow, harrow, break the clods and sow. Harness the ard to the ox, herd the sheep without a dog, feed the chickens. It is a miracle that I even managed to plant some turnips. I can barely work the handmill, that stone is so heavy. If Jak-Ur were up here, he could help with all that. Or I have to go to the town, and I've never been there. I have to tell them about the barbarians and the raid, and they'll save me. They'll give me twelve children or banish me like the witch. But what about their priest? I have to think up something. What if he told them before he left where he was going? They'll come asking. My mind is on fire with all those thoughts at night, and I can't get any sleep. That's why I see the witch; she comes after midnight. I am still awake, she waits there, next to the parsnip field.

I can go ask her for help. She is a healer; I need something for my mind. She saved my life once; maybe she will again. Maybe tomorrow.

It is the same dream again. The rag doll is a grown woman, my size, and she walks away from the sheepfold and toward the beech. She doesn't even walk; she hovers close to the mud, barefoot and with no toes. That's not strange; she never had toes, she is a rag doll. She holds a sickle. I run behind her; she turns and gives me half a stare with one of her chicken blood eyes. "You painted too much life on those cheeks of mine, Sarah," she says in a shrill voice and then vanishes in the wood. I look over the two-foot stone wall of the sheepfold; the bodies are all chopped up, as if a thousand sickles fell on them. All except for Nana. I wake up shivering. It is the autumn night of *All The Dead* and I am all alone.

Children

VI.
Ninestar

Thirteenth Winter. The Sieve. Third Night.

"O Goddess sweet and beautiful, come listen…your children…bring the light…" The words, I forget. Never could I remember the prayers, the songspells of the Goddess of light. Not even in the darkness, when I needed them most.

In the foggy darkness, my defeated rivals, no more than shadows shorter than I, began to gather. I was the first to make it to the field. Across from me, two golden eyes beamed through the bare trees and two wings, sharp as blades, spread left and right. The silver light of Selene colored the monster approaching.

"Demon," I cried.

The eagle owl found a spot on a cut trunk next to me, and his angry hoots greeted the children.

Not many breaths passed until I heard a vicious snarl, and this time it was indeed a monster. The eagle owl took flight. A dark four-legged creature was coming toward me with an unceasing steady growl, as if it had a curdled gob of spit trapped in its throat. The torchlight illuminated its head. The beast's eyes, like shining chestnuts, mirrored my tremble. It wasn't the four gleaming fangs that weakened my knees. It was the smaller teeth, so many and so sharp, lining the beast's mouth. As the torchlight flickered, the mauler's slow breath came out warm on my balls and froze me still. The dog stopped growling, bent its head, and licked my toes.

"You still smell of horseshit," Atares said with the first laughter I had heard in two days.

I was counting torches as the Guides were lighting them, around the field. They were about as many as the eyes of Darhul. The light from each torch moved differently, but together they were one dance, one circle of death around us.

I stood between Malan and Elbia, but Old Man ordered her five bodies farther. Our fingers briefly touched as she slowly walked away. Atares said with a muffled voice, "Stop, or they'll throw you into the river."

The Sheep stood among us, and we were all there again as in the previous night. Only Ughi was missing.

"They don't know, do they? They still think the first boy dies," asked Atares.

"Or the first girl," said Malan.

I heard a little girl next to Elbia. She was crying, coughing, and screaming, all together.

"I don't want to fall first."

Elbia took her hand and whispered something into her ear. I didn't hear it, but it calmed the girl. Maybe she told her not to fear because they wouldn't kill the first to fall. Or just simply, "Be strong." Elbia surely knew what to tell her.

"The second trial begins. Stand a Wolf today, and you'll feast on roast meat," the Reghen announced.

"Didn't they give you meat last night?" I asked the weakling who stood to my right.

He gave me a blank stare as if he understood nothing of what I said.

"Did you get any gruel this morning?" I asked.

It took him many breaths to give me an answer, and I wondered for a moment if the Guides had cut out the tongues of the Sheep.

He finally stuttered, "Yes."

It would have been so much easier if they hadn't given them even that. Without food, they wouldn't last even till noon.

The trial continued unchanged. We stood in the darkness, in the first breath of dawn, and then through the soft rain. I kept an eye out for the dogs, the frozen rage, and the veiled Witches—anything that could attack me. Nothing. It was easier than the first day. A handful of children fell a little after daybreak.

"You can all go to the demons. I can live without meat." With those words, Atares knelt and then crushed on the mud. It was the first surprise of the second day; his voice was not weary, he didn't even look tired.

Atares talked too much, and he was curious. He may have wanted to go to the other tents, those with the many children. He would have more Stories to tell there, I thought.

Bako did not fall, nor did Malan. My mind went back to the blade fight, Bako beating me easily in the tent the previous night. In there, I was the orphan, the one who didn't know anything. But here, outside in the mud, I was the Wolf.

And how could I not be? That was how the old Greentooth raised me since I could walk, each day harder than the one before. Not enough mare's milk, plenty of kicks and curses, and two pails to fill. The only thing that ever changed was the season: the cold that froze me to the bone, rain like needles, and heat that almost melted my skin. The day was rarely good. When it was, it was worse because the other children were out playing. Insults and stones were flying.

"Stay away, you filthy mongrel."

"Take your flies and get lost."

Each pail was heavy as a two-wintered baby, and Sirol was endless on foot. I had marked the camp from end to end. From the eastern end of the bootmakers' tents to the western end of the Archers' camp, next to the Endless Forest. But I still didn't know how to count more than a few times on my fingers.

I counted sunlight. On my eleventh winter, when I was strong enough, I figured that if I walked fast all of a day's daylight, without even stopping for a breath, I could cross once from east to west all of Sirol. My legs and hands were iron. My mind could go blank all day, working as a mule. These trials of the Sieve were silly chores. How much I wanted to shout to the Reghen, the Guides, and the Ouna-Mas: "This is too easy for me. I will never fall!"

I didn't.

Neither the Guides nor the dogs harmed the first child who fell on the second day. Nor did they harm any of the other weaklings. The Guides were no longer a threat; the other children were.

Roast meat every night. I wanted to scream with joy. By full-moon night, I would be a true fearless warrior, faster and stronger than the mauler; bite him in the neck. Victory messes quickly with the head of a twelve-wintered boy.

The day was passing under light rain and the stares of the weak. The rain added to the boredom. It stopped late in the afternoon, and a rapid cold came from the Forest. The cold tired me only a bit, while others were shivering from head to feet.

Old Man approached us. His face was so close to mine that I had to take a step back.

"Why do they fall?" he asked.

No answer.

"Who will tell me?" He was louder, closer.

"They're weaklings."

"They're Sheep. Their knees melt," said Bako.

"It's the hunger."

"The cold."

Some of those who had fallen were strong-built children.

"And not only," said Old Man.

"You? Orphan?" Now he was asking me.

"What?"

"Will you fall?"

"Never."

He turned his back on me.

I was the strongest. I wasn't meat for the dogs. I had eaten well the previous night.

When only seven of us were left, early in the evening, I raised my fist to celebrate. The rest followed—except for Malan. He just looked at me like I was a fool. None of the Reghen made a move to bring us meat. I put my arm down, and we all continued to stand.

Six remained. The Reghen did not move. Then we were five. Nothing. It was late in the evening, and all the birds had disappeared. If anything moved among the branches, it was either wolves or, worse still, Reekaal. I had never been this close to the Forest at night before as I had these first two days.

And if two of us were left? Or one?

And if only Bako and I remained, that swine with the burnt cheek? How I wanted to be alone with him in this field, without blades, to fight bare-handed.

And if it was only Malan and I? Could I take him?

If it was Elbia and I? I didn't want to fight with Elbia. She was a girl. What glory could I enjoy in that?

There was another one still standing, who I later learned was named Matsa. A Sheep who had no meat the night before. He was thin but not weak, each curve of his small muscles outlined as if he were a skinned rabbit.

Bako fell. Four of us remained.

The Reghen approached with a basket. The smell of meat.

I jumped around Bako, who was eating mud facedown, unconscious.

"You wanna fight, mudface? Get up. Come on, blade fight. Wake up, stupid. Don't be afraid," I yelled until they loaded him onto the cart.

Old Man came from the side and slapped me so hard in the head that I fell on my ass. The fresh blow woke me up. I had forgotten what my skin felt like all day. My meat was in the mud. He was shouting into my ear, almost ripping it out with two fingers. "Listen, fool. Don't ever tempt the Goddess. She saw you, she heard you."

He let me go, and I ran to Elbia. She had remained standing, a Wolf, like me. The biggest smile was carved on my face.

"He is helping me," I told her.

"Who?"

"That old Guide. The one who took me out of the tent the first night."

"I don't like the other cloudy-eyed one," she said.

I found the last remaining clothes under the shed and dressed, still lost in my smile. Those weren't my clothes. The trousers were shorter. The coat was tighter, and it stayed open around the chest. It didn't have my smell on it. It smelled of defeat. They were bad luck, these clothes. As soon as I put them on, the Goddess saw me. I stuck my tongue out at her all day, her rage would be soon coming.

I was walking toward the Wolves' tent. Its hides were an earth color, and bull horns were tied on a stake outside. Gray hides covered the other tents to the left of me, those of the Sheep, and a staked donkey's head stood in front of them. It was still dripping. To fend off the Reekaal.

We were just four children victorious in the tent, and it seemed enormous. The meat was even tastier. And more plentiful.

Elbia wiped her hands well on her trousers. "How do you do it, Da-Ren? Yesterday, they called you *meat for the dogs*, yet here you are again a second night."

I wanted to tell her the truth. *I imagine the mud to be horseshit.*

But lies came out of my mouth. "Roast meat? I will be here every night."

In a Tribe of carved monsters with iron-hard faces, she was the most beautiful. Her legs strong, not as a chicken, her brown hair shining like the tail of an Archer's horse, her full lips like double-curved bows. And those bright, fiery sparks of her eyes foretelling that our Tribe would conquer the world.

"How do you do it?" I asked her.

A smirk. That was a smirk on her lips. How did I dare to ask?

"They came to our tent the day I was born, Ouna-Mas and Reghen. He said to my mother that I was marked for glory. I was born fortunate, and I carry this prophecy with me out there in the field every morning."

It was the most fitting answer. She was the daughter of Enaka.

"You, Matsa?"

He hadn't opened his mouth except to gape upon entering the Wolves' tent. I didn't ask what the Sheep's tent was like. It was bad luck to go looking for defeat.

"I want to be an Archer."

He knew what he wanted. I still didn't.

"You, Malan?" Elbia asked him.

He didn't raise an eye to look at her. He was looking at me.

"Nothing."

"What do you mean?"

"I don't think of anything."

"Another moon. When we are done here, I'll go see my mother again," said Elbia.

She was looking only at me, once again.

I had no strength for any more talk. The sweet sleep of victory embraced me. I dreamed of a headless donkey trampling over Bako's face and belly.

Midnight, I woke to the touch of pain and the sound of my own scream. A cinder had jumped from the fire and landed on my chest. It managed to burn a hole through the woolen tunic and was scorching my bare chest underneath. That cinder wanted to wake me.

I threw it away, and my gaze fell onto the two Guides in our tent. They were sitting in front of the fire, stealing its warmth, with their backs turned. They turned for an instant when I cried out, caught a glimpse of me, and showed me their backs again. The other three children were rolled up in deep sleep. I wrapped myself with the hide and closed my eyes, but the burn on my chest and the Guides' words had woken me for good.

They talked as if I weren't there.

"We should have patched our tent before the Sieve. It leaks every night," said Murky Eyes.

"Just as well. There's only four left today, so there's enough room in here for us. The fire is bigger here. Rest and eat," answered Old Man.

"Third winter in the Sieve. A cursed fate. Where are the raids we used to go on, Rouba?"

Rouba! I knew the name of the old man who kept helping me.

"It's too late for us, Keko. We won't be raiding anymore. We have only the Sieve," answered old Rouba. His hair was gray and thinning.

"This is shit here. Minding, killing children."

"Yeah, there's no joy in this. But you know what the Reghen say."

"Better go to battle with eight wolves…"

"Than ten sheep. This is the Truth of the Sieve, two out of ten perish. It has to be so, Enaka demands the purge."

They had a slice of meat. One would take a bite and pass it to the other.

"Can you believe that these two are from the orphans? Who would have thought it?"

I tried not to make a sound. The fire stole their words and carried them up to the smoke hole, and I lost them. But when the dogs weren't barking outside, I could make out what they were saying.

"You are new to the Sieve, Keko. I have seen it many times. It is a great strength. Those who don't have a mother don't cry, don't care."

"And they don't fall."

"Yes. Look at that kid, Da-Ren. Have you seen how he stands, like his legs were tree trunks rooted to the ground? He may not fall for the entire Sieve."

"No one has ever done that."

"Oh, but he is strong. I tell you, he has passed his twelfth winter and we've forgotten him."

I lowered the hide beneath my ears so I could hear.

"With so many buckets of shit that he's carried, yes, he is strong. But those brown curls of his hair. His mother was an othertriber for sure."

"Well, lucky for him that she no longer lives," said Rouba. He turned to look at me, and I just managed to close my eyes.

"Have you seen the other one, that Malan? Whenever I turn my back, I fear he'll stab me with a knife."

"He has the eyes of the Reekaal. The Cyanus."

"Do not bring the Reekaal into the tent at night. The nights belong to the demons, and they can hear."

The Reekaal, the legendary otherworldly demons of the Endless Forest, did not steal my attention. I wanted to hear about me.

"Do you think we may be rearing the future Leader here?" asked Keko.

"Of one of the warrior Packs? For sure. But of the whole Tribe? The One? The next Khun? There are more than forty other fields with other children in the Sieve scattered around us."

"But we chose the strongest children here."

"Even so. How many winters has it been? I am an old man, and Khun-Taa is still the Leader of the Tribe. Twenty-five winters now. And there are so many others, older than they are, waiting to be Khun."

"And if we have a woman Leader growing here? Leader in a Pack? The Archers? That Elbia?"

"You know that one of these three has the curse of the Goddess. It is always the strongest of the Wolves who carries it. Second-day standing—"

"It is not Elbia. Da-Ren has the curse," Keko said.

Something was walking on my foot, but I didn't dare move. Matsa was mumbling in his sleep, and the Guides stopped talking for a few breaths.

"How do you know?" asked Rouba.

"On the first day when Sah-Ouna approached him first. Didn't you see? The mark is well hidden by his hair, but…"

The dogs kept howling outside, and I wished for lightning to burn them. I closed my eyes and played dead as the Guides turned toward me again. I tried to breathe as if I were asleep.

"What mark?" asked Rouba.

"He's a *ninestar*. I don't know how he can still be alive or what he is even doing here. But Da-Ren has the curse for sure. The third day is dawning today. Count. On exactly the twenty-first day, the Ouna-Mas will finish him."

"A ninestar and an orphan?"

I remained frozen when Rouba's fingers passed through my hair. They were warm from the fire.

"Black livers of Darhul. That's a solid mark."

"What is it?"

"He is not just a ninestar. He has the mark of the full red triangle. See, here. A cursed ninestar," said Rouba.

He took his hands away. Keko's hands also searched through my hair. They were rough, like blade stones, grinding the bones beneath my skin.

"A full red triangle. Mark of the darkness," Keko said.

"Careful you don't wake him."

"He's sleeping like a rock on the banks of the Blackvein. He won't wake. They're all dead tired."

"A true ninestar. I've never seen one in the Sieve. Not one in the ten thousand Archers when I was there."

"No one would ever make it alive that far. It takes another five springs of training to join the Archers. Black fate. What demon took the mother's mind to bear him a ninestar? Couldn't she hold another night? Or push sooner?"

I wanted to get up, ask, yell, shake them up, but I didn't. They would hear my heartbeat. They'd know I wasn't asleep. I was a "ninestar." And worse, I had no idea what that meant. The Greentooth always told me, "You won't last even nine nights in the Sieve, you cursed creature." She never said seven or ten. Always nine.

"What punishment does his mother deserve? Would you slaughter her if you knew her?"

"Slaughter her? I would nail her to a stake. Is that why Sah-Ouna spat on him first?" asked Keko.

"Why else? Sah-Ouna knows the fates of us all and every breath that comes out of our mouths till the day we die. Who do you think marked him as a baby? The Ouna-Mas."

"Stupid of you, Rouba. Why did you bring him in this pack? With the strong?"

"You shut up. The Goddess decides," said Rouba.

I had forgotten to breathe for some time.

"Wake them up. It's time for them to go out."

The other three woke and ate their gruel quickly. I couldn't swallow any, as if the mush were made of river gravel. I felt a tickling like a scorpion running up my ankle. It was only a small shiny green stinkbug warming itself near the fire. I'd eaten stink bugs many times when hunger was cutting me in half. In the orphans' tents. Where my mother had abandoned me. Whoever my mother was.

VII.
No Mother

Island of the Holy Monastery, Thirty-Third Summer.
According to the Monk Eusebius.

An eternal traveler am I, my sandals walk upon all the empires of mortal Kings, but only in the Empire of Heaven do I belong.

And now, as I write the story of Da-Ren, nowhere will I make mention of the name of his tribe, or the names of our Empire and its Emperors as they have already been written down in history. Because this is not the epos of one tribe, of the straw-haired, or the brown-skinned, or the blue-eyed, or the slanted-eyed, or the black-haired. It is not the story of a tribe of the north or the east whose feet once thundered upon the earth before obliterating itself, a victim of its own barbarism. This is a story of every tribe's rightful thirst for survival, and its lawless hunger for the annihilation of its neighbors. God has not cursed or embraced one tribe alone; anyone may sit to the right or to the left of Him.

And I will make no mention of the dates of the historical age because it is the story of every age from the time that Man made the knife, sharpened it, fastened it to his belt, and fought the abominable beasts and his own *despair with his Brother as comrade. Until the time when Woman came between them and the Brothers turned on each other. And Woman planted in their place the seed of the next Man, the better, the stronger.*

And I will not refer to the empires and the cities with the names that all remember still. I will intentionally wash them clean, for I can bear none of them, nor omit them from my story, nor write their true names. They are the names of all the cities that fell, and will fall again, into the hands of the barbarians. Even those that still stand unconquered will fall in time. For it is all of these cities, ours and theirs, that deserve to weep for this story. And it is all the fiery deserts, the endless grasslands of the steppe, and the darkest forests made of timber and of stone; these are the wombs that spat out the barbarians and will do so again.

No, I will not mention all this because I am a man of God, still, and this is not my world. I am only passing. My world is eternal, there above in the heavens—neither north nor east have I a curse to cast, neither south nor west do I have to offer praise.

Already fourandten days had passed since I had commenced on the documentation of Da-Ren's story. The elder monks had decreed that it was to be I who took on the task of the scribe.

"The wisdom of the monk is within his cell, in his solitude, and a great sin indeed it would be for one of the Elders of advanced age to hear the profligate memories of this barbarian," said the First Elder.

"You are a young novice. You will have all the time to repent, and this tedious task will also serve as your penance," they explained.

I am eternally grateful to their fear and their laziness.

Da-Ren had been for a year on Hieros Island before he was persuaded to tell me his story. He had spent those months in chains, then exchanging pleas and curses, and finally with ample study of the holy and other books. He was neither a monk nor a novice, nor would he ever become one until all his unholy deeds had been documented. The monks expected him to suffer for his sins, repent, and receive forgiveness. He would accomplish only the first.

He did not attend the holy service, but we offered him food, clothing, and lodging. In exchange, he would fish, carry stones for the walls and the church and other supplies from the cove up to the monastery. The idle receive no food, and the lazy deserve no warm clothes, not even at the Holy Monastery. This was an inviolable rule.

I had taken it upon myself to try to teach him our language as best I could. He could speak quite a few sentences but could not write a single word. I explained to him that I would begin to write down his story only when I deemed him ready in language and mind. He agreed to all these terms because of the assurance the monks had given him that this would save his wife and daughter.

It was the kind of story that one would never read in a monastery. After many years of study, I knew well the language of the saints and the sages and the writings of east and west, but I could not understand even the simplest truths of his tribe. There in the north, between the steppe and the North River, Blackvein he called it, was a world of agony, dark and barbarous, a hell deep within the bowels of the earth.

At first, he believed that we would finish in no more than a few weeks. Initially, I shared that belief and expected him to recite a brief story about his wife and daughter and how their lives were in mortal danger. But I knew nothing of his tribe and every answer he gave me, brought up more questions. At the end of the second week, he asked me if it was necessary to describe with such exhausting detail his childhood years.

I answered, "The elder monks asked you to tell me everything that you saw and lived. Everything, Da-Ren, every pagan custom and any sacrilegious acts."

I did not know what sacrilegious acts a boy of twelve could commit and what purpose it served to waste so much papyrus and time stolen from my prayers to write this sinful barbaric tale. But these indeed had been their words to me.

It was worse than any rumor ever heard of these tribes. A man of God would never read it, and it would not lead me closer to the gates of Heaven, but to the jaws of Hell. And we were only at the beginning.

Baagh wanted me to stretch the documentation of the story as long as possible, make it as long and detailed as I could, and I tried to do it without exhausting the patience of the barbarian. It wasn't hard, as we haven't even started getting into the heart of his tale.

We always met in his bare cell; he sat on the stone floor or the straw mat, I on the stool behind the writing desk. It was never hot in there, not even in summer, the stone walls remained chilly as his story, the small window open to the sea winds and the salty rain. Winter was torture even for a monk, the bone-piercing dampness punished me for every stroke of ink.

"Da-Ren, for a year now you have been pleading for your wife and daughter's life, but you have yet to speak even a single word of them."

"I did not fall in love with my wife at thirteen, Eusebius. I could never—"

"But I thought that Elbia—"

"That was impossible. You don't understand."

"That which I fail to understand is how the powerful of your tribe could accept exposing their noble-born children to the same trials as the orphaned and the poor. How could any mother tolerate this atrocity against the more privileged—"

"The *what* born? You have indeed grasped very little."

"I too have never known my parents, but all the scriptures say family is sacred and parents should never abandon their—"

"No child knew their parents, Eusebius. There was no marriage in the Tribe."

"How can that be? You said that Elbia's mother—"

"The women and children stayed together until the child's twelfth winter. That could have been Elbia's mother raising her, then again it may not have been. Whoever she was, she was raising many other children from the same tent at the same time together with other mothers, whether they were hers or not. Any woman with a childless belly and on her feet, would do. If you were lucky enough to have the same woman as a mother for a long time, it simply meant that she was not getting pregnant. And then, barren and useless, she could end up floating face up in the Blackvein along the slave corpses, kissing the vultures."

"Godless words."

"Only few could be sure of their true mothers. And no one ever knew who fathered them. Each child had to make up a Legend about his father, a Legend that lifted our blades when our hands could not. No child, from any tent, ever knew who his father was. No woman belonged to one man. A man could have a child with any woman. He would fuck anyone, always from behind to give birth to boys."

I made the sign of the cross.

Behind our monastery on the western side of the island lay the few mud huts of the villagers who coexisted peacefully with us on this salt-ravaged rock. They would provide us with food and other necessary supplies, and in turn we offered them God's blessings, their only protection from pirate raids. The First Elder charged me with the task of collecting supplies from the villagers, so I had seen many women. Some were filthy and miserable, looking like the daughters of Satan, but others kept my gaze engaged longer than it should have been.

The First Elder cautioned me early, when the first hair of manhood appeared on my upper lip, "Resist the temptation of the flesh, go to your cell, and pray. The cell will be your teacher and your only guide."

But my cell would soon become the altar of impiety, as Da-Ren's savage and licentious tales crawled down dark, lowly paths.

"Let me tell you about my mother, Eusebius. My mother was the horse dung fire of the tent. The fire nurtured me. And my father was a Legend. I will tell you his Legend someday, the Legend I made up for him. And that was the same for all of us, orphan or not."

"That's unspeakable cruelty."

"No, it was very easy. This age-old agreement made my Tribe as hard as iron and as invincible as the wind."

"To struggle in vain."

"To struggle only for the glory of the Tribe. We had brothers. Thousands of brothers. All equal. What is cruel and difficult is having a family."

"No mother waits for her child to return from the Sieve," I answered.

"And no mother bade her child farewell. Even if it was of her blood when the child left for the Sieve, never to be seen again."

I never had, nor ever believed it my fate to have, my own family. But this barbarism made me rise from my stool and stop writing.

"Now do you understand, Eusebius, why…I never…"

Da-Ren faltered. Was it possible for one of these barbarians to weep?

He lifted himself from the cold stone floor where he had remained cross-legged for quite some time. With his forehead and left palm, he supported himself on the decaying wall next to the window. His right fist pounded the wall seven times. He had done it before, and every time he hit the wall seven times. The white lime cracks were splattered with red spots as Da-Ren found his words again. "Do you understand now why I cannot speak to you of my wife and daughter before you learn that no one in our Tribe was permitted to even have a wife and daughter? You have to understand that, Eusebius, or else you are going to write shit for a story."

And with that, he bade me to leave him with a flip of his hand, without even raising his head to look at me. For the entire night during prayer and matins at the break of dawn, I could not concentrate on my invocations. I feared that I may have locked him into his other cell, the one of his darkest mind, and he would abandon the telling altogether. The next morning after the service, I went to him and asked him to continue as he saw fit.

"Tell me, Da-Ren. What did the Guides mean when they said that you were a ninestar? What curse was this?"

"At last, a good question, monk."

Apocrypha IV.
Come Back, Come Back

As the One Mother heard the Legends, Chapter IV

No spiders, flies, or worms. None of them come near the well anymore. It may be the cold; it may be that Jak-Ur is lying down there like a sick dog that has accepted his fate. He will rot and die if he doesn't move.

He heard the priest's mule whinny so I had to do something. I harnessed the ropes to the mule, and it pulled and pulled. It pulled Jak-Ur up ten feet, and he could climb higher. I had to cut the rope; he didn't see me doing that. He can't come out, but I don't want him to die either.

We started to draw together. Whenever the hand gestures fail us, we use wood and charcoal, and we try to draw. We put the wooden tablet in the bucket and pass it up and down to each other. *He* tries mostly.

He drew a horse. I shook my head "no."

He drew a wheel and an axle. Every well should have one. I was surprised at that; I didn't think those barbarous dogs could build machines. I shook my head "no."

He drew a deer, but how could I ever yoke a deer and a mule together to pull his weight? Maybe what he meant was he was hungry. He seems to have shriveled to half his size, parsnips and turnips, turnips and parsnips his only punishment.

He drew something that looked like a priest with a hat and robe—or a long-haired woman wearing a dress—pushing him down the well. I am not sure what he drew. I know he didn't see me that first day, it all happened so fast. Does he know? I shook my head "no."

He drew an ox. I have one, though he doesn't know it. I shook my head.

I made a drawing of wolves and trees. I am going into the wood to find the witch's hut. Sooner not later I'll have to make a decision. He drew a hide, and I sent down a woolen cape and a hide; the clothes of the dead will keep him warm but not for long. Every year, the cold gets unbearable after the night of All The Dead, as if they exhale it from their graves to our huts.

He will die by the next moon, freeze to death at night, dreaming of horse, deer, and woman. Is he dreaming of me? It is not a satisfying end, not the revenge I crave.

There is a basket filled with round gourds in the witch's hut; they have the color of a man's skin. I thought they were skulls when I first saw them.

She hasn't looked much at me since she let me in her abode. She knows I need help.

"Atropos, Atropos to witness your fate," she mumbles.

If you could learn your fate from eating these black berries, you wouldn't be here, witch. I think it, but I don't say it.

"Lolum, lolum, boil it to make a man your slave," she whispers.

If you could make men your slaves with this weed, they wouldn't have banished you here, poor woman.

She is not even twice my age, yet she is scrawny, white-haired and wrinkled. A tuft of black hair grows on her left forearm. I remembered her different. There is a smaller hut next to hers, much smaller. Maybe it can fit a child lying down, or a rag doll standing up. It is made of stone and mud and is surrounded by bleeding heather shrubs. It seems much sturdier than hers, meant to keep a secret inside, something that shouldn't come out. It doesn't have doors or windows.

She should hate me; I am one of them, I am the daughter of the one who exiled her here, the one who wouldn't acknowledge her bastard baby.

And yet she is the only one who ever saved me, other than myself. I was thirteen years old, it was an autumn eve, and I wandered in the wood. Most of the daylight was gone when I came upon the rivulet. Under the oak tree, the wolves were tearing the young deer apart. Their hides were gray, white, and black, their muzzles scarlet, crimson, and amaranth. The largest, a black one, turned his yellow eyes on me. He crossed the rivulet, growling.

The witch almost jumped out of the trunks, stepped in front of me and started to shout at the beast. I shut my eyes, I heard the wolves fighting, and when I opened them again, the black wolf lay there bleeding next to the dead deer. The deer had munched the last green leaves of the tree. The wolf had torn apart the deer. The tree's roots were already feeding on the wolf's carcass, awaiting spring. It was autumn, just like now, a tree, a wolf, a deer. All three of them so beautiful and carmine, one embrace.

She had said the same thing back then.

"Come back, come back."

"What do I do? What do I do?" I ask the witch.

I always repeat things twice as she does, it makes the answers come faster. We are out of time. I have left Jak-Ur alone for two days and nights—he has water, but no meat or bread. I want to bring tears to his eyes when he sees me; I am close, I will make the savage cry.

The witch gives me the belladonna's poison in the wooden cup to sip. My mother said that whoever eats the black berries will go blind. I wish I could be blind only when I chose, but not forever. The witch speaks, staring into the cauldron where she stirs and boils:

You do not take the life from this wolf;
You bring the light to the well.
You do not push fear down the hole;
You face fear with eyes open.
You do not kill a man with iron and fire;
You kill him with wine and song.
You do not take revenge by murdering the weakest;
You take revenge by bleeding them all.

"Was that you? Did you guide those murderers all the way to our hamlet from the river?"

She just looks out her one window. All she can see from there is the small stone tomb, her only view. Not even the heather shrubs.

But I have good reason to ask. You see, I walked up the path that the barbarians descended from the other day, reached half way to the hill from which I can see the Northern River. I wanted to see if they left anyone behind. Mother. I found the clothes of our men and children, and the bones of a pig ripped apart and cut into pieces. Like someone created a two-days' ride scent trail for the dogs to find our settlement.

"Was that you, witch? Look at my eyes; not out there."

"Lola, lola to make a man your slave," she whispers.

"You don't have magic. Couldn't save yourself or my brother," I scream and run away. "Die in here, that's what you deserve."

"Come back, come back," she says.

I run out the door and don't look back.

Much later I'll realize that she doesn't order or beg me. She knows I'll come back. She is a fortune-teller, it is a prophecy.

I sleep alone in the longhouse; the sheep bleat in fright every time I scream in my sleep. They wake me up; the sheep, the screams, the dreams. She comes back, comes back in my dreams.

You do not have any magic, and yet they all fear you.

You could not save anyone, and yet you saved me.

You have never seen Jak-Ur, and yet you know what I must do.

You do not have a knife, yet you slaughtered them all.

That is power. Not my father with his swords, not Jak-Ur and his bow and quiver. Not the priest and his God. Not Crispus and his chestnut hairlocks. The Witch is power.

I envy you; I must become you, I will become you.

I will come back. You knew that already.

You will teach me everything, and I'll believe nothing.

I am standing above the well again, and the moon is full. But it will change soon; angry clouds are coming from the forest. They were already there, but I ran faster than them.

It will snow tomorrow.

The moonlight pours a cauldron of liquid hope down the well.

I take the wood and the charcoal. I press the coal hard, to show in the scant moonlight.

I draw an ox.

I lower the bucket with the drawing.

He kneels.

Maybe he cries, maybe it's the moonlight in his eyes.

VIII.
Even When the Stars

Thirteenth Winter. The Sieve. Third Day.

I collapsed like a sack of bones in the mud on that third morning. Rouba and Keko's night whispers were dripping in my head like poison. They followed me from the moment I stood in the field till the mud embraced me.

"Ninestar. I have never seen one in the Sieve…marked by the Ouna-Mas. Da-Ren is sure to have the curse of Enaka. It is the third night today. They will finish him on the twenty-first day. Why do we keep him and feed him meat?"

For the first time, I got inside the head of every child who had fallen and lived their nightmares. I was cold, but I didn't fall from the cold. I was hungry, but I didn't fall from hunger. My knees hurt, but they didn't bring me down.

Defeat crawled up from the dark well of my mind, where the tongues of the two Guides were stirring the curses and the ninestar marks. Defeat found me.

"Why do the weak fall?" Rouba came and asked again, as he had the day before.

I didn't answer.

"Speak, you rats."

Their legs burn out, the hunger pierces their bowels, the cold cracks their bones. That's what they would tell him.

"You? Orphan?" Again, he asked me.

They didn't fall because of tiredness, hunger, or cold. They fell because they didn't believe in victory anymore. Defeat had taken hold of their minds. Their hearts burned out way before their legs.

I didn't answer.

"Will you fall? Are you Wolf or Sheep?"

I didn't answer. I just wanted to sit for a while, to rest. Just for one breath.

I made the same rounds with my eyes under the first rays of sunlight, but more carefully this time. Sooner or later, I would have to find an escape before the twenty-first day. On each side were sheds that stored the hay bushels, but there were also some for the Guides and their horses to take cover. The Reghen and the Ouna-Mas were not there. Afterward, I learned how to smell death creeping up on us, whenever I saw an Ouna-Ma.

The Wolves' and the Sheep's tents were on the south side of the field. Those of the Guides were on the west. A wall of naked oaks stood along the western and northern edges. Before dawn, we could still hear the monsters of the Forest howling. On the other two sides of the camp, stood adjacent sheds that protected bushels of hay and, behind them rose a thick prickly hedge bush, barren of green, a fence of thorns. Once or twice we'd heard children's screams, dogs barking behind the wall of thorns.

We were trapped in a cage surrounded by Guides and maulers. The dogs would catch my scent in an instant. They would find me before I even had the chance to run out of Sirol. And go where? I had never left Sirol before.

I started fighting my own mind. Defeat had taken control of it.

It's early. The day has just broken, I thought.

I'm tired, my mind answered back.

Not even three have fallen yet. We have to hold on.

Ninestar, it mumbled.

One boot stepped into my mind, another on my heart, and they were thrusting me downward. I took two steps behind the line as if that would be enough to hide from them. I fell, and my knees sank into the shit-colored mud. I pressed hard with my hands and let out a nervous giggle as my foot slipped back. I got on one knee and pushed again in vain. I was face down on the brown mud. It was daybreak when I fell. I remember that, nothing else.

I didn't dream of anything. A cauldron pouring darkness.

Two small hands wrapped themselves tightly around me, and the sound of children's coughing woke me. A little girl with curly hair had cuddled behind me. She was a twelve-wintered but half my size. I was in a small tent with many other children packed like sheep who smelled of puke and piss all together under the same hides. *Packed like Sheep.* I could make out Urak and Matsa, but not Malan or Elbia. Unlike me, those two had remained Wolves for the third straight day. Three of the children were coughing and wouldn't stop even to take a breath. Their days were ending. I had seen many orphans withering away every winter.

We walked out of the tent. A large pot was standing there, its fire long gone. Before I even got close to it, countless small hands were dipping inside. I was the last to reach it, so only fresh rain and a bit of gruel remained at the bottom. I dipped both my hands to take as much as I could, to scrape the dregs from the bottom of the pot, and I licked my fingers clean. No one had eaten meat here. I could smell the stinking hands of the other children in my gruel.

When I reached the field of trials, Malan approached and asked me, "How is it?"

He never spoke first or much until then, but he wanted to taste my defeat.

"It's like hunger," I answered.

"Don't they have any?"

He was talking about roast meat.

"They don't have Story," I answered.

Elbia, Malan, Bako, and Danaka were walking toward me from the Wolves' side, looking strong, tall, and fed. The night before, they roasted horse meat and talked around the fire. I could guess their words: *Sheep, fall, Da-Ren, weakling.* It was my flesh that they ripped and roasted.

The fourth day dawned on her face.

They don't have Elbia.

They have tears and puke.

It was only when Elbia's worried eyes fell on me that I knew what I had to do: find the Truth of the Ouna-Ma, of the twenty-first day. I couldn't even count that far.

My belly was empty, but my legs were hard as iron once more. I was hungry for the Story. Elbia walked past me, our palms touched and she left something in mine. Meat, a small piece.

"I kept some for you," she whispered.

I swallowed quickly before the Guides could see me.

We were lined up again. All children, seven times the fingers of my one hand, each two paces apart from the other. The wind had changed. It swept through the bare trees from the north, colder than the days before. The dogs sauntered around us. They had not killed again.

Afternoon came, and we were seven, bone cold, but the Reghen did not throw meat. The Sun was setting red, his sky-archers aiming the last bloodied arrows on us. Malan fell, then Elbia, then it was only Urak and I. He was hungry too. The Guides still wouldn't stop us. Selene came out half and growing hunchbacked, and I shook my head toward Urak.

"No. Not today."

Even if we had stayed out there until the moon was full, five nights later, I would still be standing. I was hungry for the Truth like a damned ninestar, whatever that was.

Urak fell like a dead mule a little later, and the two Guides took me to the Wolves' tent all alone, as if I were the one Leader of all. Keko tripped twice on the way, his stare frozen on me. He was searching for my ninestar mark. He could see only my triumph.

There were some leftover clothes in the hut, but they weren't mine. I'd swear that I could smell Elbia's hair on the hide that covered me.

I ate a huge piece of juicy meat. The largest of any day, as if it were for five children and they had forgotten to cut it into pieces. I saved some for the next morning. I was all alone in the tent and asked Rouba, "Will they come?"

"Who?"

"The Reghen, the Ouna-Ma."

"They always come. They will be late. Sleep."

I dreamed of Malan and Elbia. They were biting each other's flesh. I dreamed of the shooting stars falling from the sky. Nothing else.

The wailing of a birthing dog woke me in the middle of the night. After a while, the Reghen, the Ouna-Ma, and the Guides came in.

I tried to open my mouth to ask, but the words would not come out. They ignored me and talked among themselves. I caught a few words: *the damned orphan* and *ninestar*. I bit my lip until it bled.

Few days were left until the twenty-first. If I didn't find the Truth, it would find me.

The Guides had brought just a wooden cup filled with goat milk. When the Reghen came close to give it to me, I lifted my hair and my ear to reveal the small red triangle.

"What is a ninestar?" I asked, with the taste of my own blood in my mouth. I would hear the Story that I wanted to hear and only that.

The Ouna-Ma turned her head sharply, removed her veil for the first time, and started whispering menacing words I couldn't decipher. The Guides, awed, took two steps back.

Her eyes. I wanted to swallow my words and my questions. Black wells of magic and despair. The pupil and the iris, pitch black, were so big that there was almost no white left in her eye. Black suns shining bright. Her hair almost shaved, cut short and angry. But it was her head, the shape of a snake egg that terrified me, the head she had always covered by the red dark veil, now naked and magical before us. Under the skin, the skull grew toward the back and upward in an otherworldly way, beautiful as a hunter's quiver. It was true, the Ouna-Mas were creatures of another world. She was like no other woman I'd ever seen.

Her thin, cold, red-painted fingers came out from beneath her robe and lifted my hair to see my mark underneath my ear. She put her veil back on, and I could see her eyes no longer. She formed a triangle with her two forefingers and two thumbs in front of her face like a shield between her eyes and my face. Then she walked out of the tent with Keko and the Reghen.

I remained alone with Rouba inside the tent.

"She cannot tell you the Truth. Only a Reghen can talk to you," Rouba said.

"Is he coming back?"

"You know, they say that even a three-wintered Ouna-Ma has the same head. Those few who have secretly seen the very young ones," he told me.

"I have never seen one so close."

"They don't live long, and the older ones are all blind and never leave their tents."

Keko and the Reghen came back into the tent. The Ouna-Ma did not return that night.

"So, you want to learn of the ninestars, Da-Ren?" asked the Reghen.

"Yes, the Legend."

"It is not a Legend. Listen to me, but ask no questions."

The Reghen spoke only for me:

The Truth of the Stars

The Dawn of Man:

The Demon ripped out his own heads, turned them into arrow-snakes and sent them onto the seventh and last Sun.

But the Goddess swallowed them all to save her endmost son. Enaka's belly soon swelled and burst into myriad fragments making the stars in the sky.

Dust fell from the stars, and from them sprouted the first men of the Tribe.

We are all from different stars and different dust but all pieces of the One Goddess.

From darkness and blinding light we are made, and only the Ouna-Mas can see the stardust in our blood, the bright star in our eyes, and our fate. They see where the light of the Goddess blinds with its golden radiance, they see where the darkness is the shadow of Darhul.

Thus declared the Ouna-Mas:

The female babies born on the night of the first full moon of spring will be taken from their mothers at once to be raised by the Ouna-Mas.

The babies, male and female, born on the seventh night after each full moon shall be marked with a circle in the hollow behind the ear because they are fortunate and will bring honor and glory to the Tribe.

You will call them sevenstar.

The male babies born nine days after the full moon will be marked with a triangle before they grow hair because they are unlucky, ninestar.

Hear the last command:

If they have been born on the ninth night after the first full moon of

Spring, nine nights after the feast of the Goddess, you will give them a full mark because their fate is far worse than the rest.

These true ninestars will bring darkness and bloodshed to the Tribe.

A black circle for the fortunate sevenstars and a red triangle for the unlucky ninestars.

You will watch them and follow them throughout every generation, because the stars are made of the flesh and blood of the Goddess, and they will never lie.

Thus declared the Ouna-Mas, the Voices of the Unending Sky.

When the Reghen finished the Story, he looked at me with eyes cold and lips tightened. Before I had a chance to ask, he spoke. *To give me courage? To get rid of me?*

"The signs say that you were born with a dark fate, but that doesn't mean that you are doomed, Da-Ren. Only Sah-Ouna knows what it means to bring glory to the Tribe. What it means to bring darkness. Or blood. Sah-Ouna deemed you worthy to face the three deaths of the Sieve. Sometimes words mean the opposite. Sometimes even these things are needed. The darkness, the blood."

"What does it mean—" I started to ask, but the Reghen spoke his last words as he left.

"Do not lose yourself in your own darkness. Fight it. If you were not needed, you would already be dead."

I prepared as a lone, unlucky Wolf, taking off my clothes for yet another day in the field. The only thing I wore was my loincloth around my waist and my ninestar mark. Already it was more than I wanted.

Rouba grabbed the back of my neck with his big hand. He had one drop of courage left to give me.

"The stars mark us all, Da-Ren. With one sign or another. But the Goddess lets us live. No matter what sign we may carry. She lets us live to prove what sign we deserve."

"She lets us live so she can laugh at us," Keko roared.

"Don't listen to him, Da-Ren. This is why we were born. This is why we live. To keep fighting even when the stars have abandoned us. And then, when our actions glow so brilliant they turn even the stars pale, only then does Enaka summon us close to her."

With those words, Rouba left me in the field again.

Countless were the glowing star-fires in the night sky. The children who had spent the night in the Sheep's tents were in the field waiting just for me. I too took my place and this time stood next to Elbia.

Keko sent her far from me before I had a chance to give her the meat that I had hidden in my palm. As she walked away, a gust of north wind blew her hair and I noticed for the first time the black circle of the lucky sevenstar marked behind her ear.

I thought I heard her whispering to me again, "Luck, I kept some for you."

It gave me the strength to carry on until the Sieve's end.

IX.
No Pyre for the Ghosts

Thirteenth Winter. The Sieve. Eighth Night.

Never again to the North.
Donned in white they stand there.
The ghosts with mulberry lips.
They show mercy for no one.
Gently, they take us in their arms,
like vile serpents wrap themselves around.
So cold the skin.
Before the break of dawn.
A death naked of screams.

It was the eighth night. The madness of the same torment repeating every morning had seeped under our skins and tied knots inside our stomachs. In the middle of the night, came a different Reghen, the third that had come in eight days, dressed exactly the same as the others.

A freezing wind was blowing off the mountain crests that rose beyond the Endless Forest. It was descending from the lands haunted by the bloodeaters and the ice-rivers that the Drakons guarded.

I remained standing for yet another day. I feasted again as a Wolf, the meat and then a Story. The Legend that the Reghen had chosen that night was of the Tribe's ancient journey to the North. Its Truth fell as a deadly chill on us that night and even worse at dawn.

The Legend of Khun-Nan's journey to the North
The Fifth Season of the World: Part One

In midsummer, the age-old Demon Darhul sent the black star with the ashen tail thundering through the Sky. Unstoppable, it crashed upon the earth and its dust swallowed the Sun. Thus began the Fourth Season, that of the Famine on the eastern steppe. Only three times a thousand, and some say fewer, survived from the entire Tribe, and even they were no more than hunched skeletons from hunger. They roamed as beggars, but no othertriber showed our people mercy.

It was then that the First Leader of the Tribe, Khun-Nan, rose to power and with him the Fifth Season of the world began, that of the Khuns.

Beside him was his blind daughter, Ouna-Ma, she who first carried the name, and the only seed that remained after he had lost his other five children to the Famine.

Enaka gave the sight of destiny to the blind one, and she commanded her father to lead our Tribe to the North.

With blood and iron, Khun-Nan persuaded the people of the Tribe to follow him to the North, the land of the Drakonsnakes. This was a long, very long time ago, before the Tribe had passed the great Eastern River, the last border of the steppe, and brought us here to the Iron Valley in Sirol.

The enemies of the First Khun foresaw death and despair. But this earth we walk upon belongs to the Goddess. She etches her wishes in the Sky, and the earth reflects them on the dirt we walk.

"We must reach the end of the North. There Enaka awaits," said the Ouna-Ma.

The Tribe continued northbound until it met with a terrible obstacle. A Drakon, crystaleyed and firecloven, scaled in ice-blades, stood guard on the only passage, the frozen river that never flowed. The Drakon had no name because no one who had been close enough to hear it ever returned.

The three brave warriors of Khun-Nan, the first three Reghen, slayed the Drakon. But that is a different Legend for a braver night. They drew fire from his belly to heal the Tribe from the cold and stole its green flesh to heal the Tribe from hunger. And they took the drakonteeth as triumphal bounty for Khun-Nan.

This is how the passage opened to the North, and the Ouna-Ma said to her father, "Take the drakonteeth, and go to the cave of white darkness at the lands' end."

So Khun-Nan ventured alone and found the Goddess Enaka waiting there for him. She had taken the shape of a doe. He offered her the drakonteeth, and she in turn gave him the weapon of victory.

The Goddess warmed him with her breath and said, "Come close, First Leader. I will teach you how to make the twohorn, the double-curved, the snake bow. With this, you will triumph in all battles. Take the heart of the strongest maple wood you can cut, and mix it with glue of the boiled horse's bones, sinew from the ox's neck, and elk's horn. Your warriors, Khun-Nan, will draw these bows with ease even in mid-gallop. They will not need to have their feet planted on the ground. Unleash its force, and you will drive the heavy iron-tipped arrow from three hundred feet away into the heart of your enemy. The lighter spruce tip will travel even a thousand."

And Khun-Nan returned to his people and said, "Now we will strike south and west, and no one will stop us. Make your quivers large, because that is where we will pour our revenge. Our arrows will fall like a rainstorm on our enemies, faster than their feet and eyes. We will blacken the sky from end to end with these bows and annihilate the othertribal demons."

This snake-curved bow, born of elk, ox, horse, and maple, was the revenge Khun-Nan had sworn for the loss of his five children. With the bow of victory, Khun-Nan rode south before the coming of the deadly winter.

The last waning moon of autumn had already passed.

"My horse and bow warriors, let's now head south to the steppe. Never again will you be beggars, and no one will be able to stop us."

But for some of them, it was already too late. Winter has no mercy for the weak. White-haired women and frail children did not survive the windswept journey of return, and their frozen corpses remain there, unburned and unkissed ghosts. There was no pyre for the ghosts, no time for Khun-Nan to light a funeral fire, and the dead of the Tribe cursed him. The children and the old stand frozen there, only their lips still whispering. Their harrowing whispers have awakened Drakons of evil power.

The Goddess never again blessed Khun-Nan with a son, even though he lay with all the iron-legged women of the Tribe who had survived. That was his punishment.

The younger women of the Tribe had all but perished in the North. Poisoned by the ashen sky that spewed fire when the black star crashed to the ground, they stopped giving birth. Only coal and dead crows grew in the bellies. One child and two women remained alive for every ten men.

The few and childless, the warriors of Khun-Nan, rode until the banks of the first easterly river carrying their strong bows, the gifts of Enaka.

The Ouna-Ma said, "You made it, Father. There they wait, across the river. The She-Wolves."

"How can you tell, my daughter?"

"I smell their warm piss, I hear their lustful howls, I taste their silent fear. Their males are weak. Cross the river, Father, and a new strong and fearless seed will take root in our Tribe."

Khun-Nan's warriors crossed the wide waters and mated with the wolfen mothers, under the light of Selene. The Tribe was reborn with strong male children born with wolfen souls.

Before the First Ouna-Ma closed her lightless black eyes to go to her One Mother, she told her people, "May no one ask about your wolfen mothers. There will be no moonlight around the pupils of your eyes or thick gray fur on your backs. From the wolves, you took the spirit and not the form. Believe that."

That is the Legend of the First Ouna-Ma and the She-Wolves who bore us all, the Legend of the First Khun, who found the bow of victory in the North.

Thus declared the Ouna-Mas, the Voices of the Unending Sky.

The Reghen ended his Story, and I moved to cuddle closer to the fire's embrace. The night was quiet and peaceful, though the wind was singing relentlessly to her with ice-blue lips. Even the dogs were quiet, hiding from the frost. I had heard it many times back at the orphans' tents during the past few moons: "A brutal winter was descending from the North." The bees had built their hives higher in the trees than ever before. The apple skins were thick and hard as pig hides that autumn. Even the birds of passage had flown south early.

As the eighth day dawned, the ghosts slipped in silence through the north wind and nailed their ice needles at the soft of our necks.

Apocrypha V.
And I Shall Come with Arms Red

As the One Mother heard the Legends, Chapter V

Clouds gather above the well and stare down at us. God has sent them to judge me. Jak-Ur will die soon if I don't face my fear.

It is my last chance because it will snow tonight. I still haven't buried the dead. A murder of crows has gathered. All other birds have disappeared. I have lost the birdsong since the day they came. If it snows, and it will, if the white sheets cover the dead then I can't burn them anymore. Not until spring. He shouldn't find them here tonight, on his first night. No one should. It is time for the fire to purge.

There is plenty of dry wood, so many huts without life.

The flames go up and up, black clouds of smoke, under black clouds of winter, reaching black clouds of crows.

One thing I never liked about the priest was his hands. He had pale yellow fingers and long dirty nails. Why does a man who never works the land have dirt under his nails? His headless corpse was the last one at the very edge of the sheepfold that refused to blaze. But he is gone now too.

It is not easy, not easy at all to yoke the ox and the mule together. Most men in the village wouldn't be able to do it, yet most men never did much. They were retired soldiers of the Empire who settled here with my father. They preferred to practice with their swords, go hunting and fishing, drink the wine, shout at their women to hurry. Always hurry. The women did most of the hard work, even the ard.

I hope it snows soon; this cloud of smoke can be seen from far away. Somebody may come and ask; somebody will come and ask. What am I doing here? Who is this barbarian that I share my longhouse with? What will I say?

The priest said a prayer when he found the dead in the barn, and I was waiting behind him. The sickle was hanging there on the supporting beam. I didn't plan it, I knew I had to do something, but the sickle helped me decide. The priest prayed above the dead:

"And He will come with wounds red, to judge the living and the dead."

Why? Why will he do that? Did we invite him? When? What does he wait for? Doesn't he listen to so many prayers, or see so many melting candles? Every spring, we slaughter our fattest sheep and sell their whitest wool to buy candles to pray for Anastasis. It never comes. Why doesn't he listen? The witch's baby burning with fever, my brother wailing, Jak-Ur above him? Mother, gone. What does he wait for? Does he enjoy the spectacle? Are we some rag dolls painted with chicken blood, jesters to fill his nights? If rain is his tears, what is snow? His indifference, his forgetfulness? White and soft?

It is time, Jak-Ur. Ten feet. You've been that far before. I can always cut the rope, but this time you hear me screaming and whipping the animals. This is our last chance ere the snow buries you tonight.

Judge me, father. Why do I help the one who murdered you, the one who raped your son and my little brother? Because if I leave him there, I am a coward, my soul is lost forever. I will never be the one who kills him face to face. He will be the fear that never leaves, I bury it deep, but his ghost will remain, and live in my head. If he stays in the hole, father, he won. He is forever the one skeleton I don't dare to face. I have to run then, find another village, a cursed lone woman, not even a virgin.

Judge me, father priest. But see, the moment I cut your throat, I was banished to hell. Now I have to walk through it, and I need an infidel dog for company.

Judge me, mother. But you didn't say a word when father promised me to the priest. I was with Crispus from first youth. He was the one for me, the boy with the long curly hair and the hands of an angel. We were to wed, he had whispered the sacred words of promise before we lay in the barn, that's why I let him, and then he touched my lips, my breasts, and my legs. He tried to do things I didn't understand until I saw Jak-Ur and little brother. It was painful, and I got no joy. He smelled good, but I drowned in guilt. I shouldn't have done it; maybe I disappointed him, I don't know. See, I'll never know. He left soon after, to join the Empire's soldiery just like my father. He disgraced me and abandoned me. Was it because God gave him a sign as he claimed? Was it because of that painful afternoon in the barn? Or was it because of the murrain? We used to have a lot more cattle, but most of them died. All that is left is the one ox that pulls now.

"Twenty feet. Almost there, Jak-Ur."

My little brother would inherit the land; my father had promised the cattle to Crispus after he wed me. The cattle fell dead last winter; I tried to save them, rubbed them with the blue-green dust, but there was nothing I could do. "God's will," you say, Mother. Crispus sees a sign of God in his sleep; he has to leave, he will never wed me.

Father says he is proud and pats him on the back. He gives him a fast horse. Father is mad at me for I should have married him by now, he says. He doesn't even know I am already given to him. I should wait for him, father says. Twenty years, he'll be back if he survives the battles. He won't. He is soft and a coward, that's why he left, he will be slaughtered like sheep in the battlefields and no God will help poor Crispus, the boy with the curly hair. I will have to wear a black veil and live from my nineteenth year a widow, never to be touched again, remaining loyal and waiting for the one who abandons me willfully, you say father. I think Mother knows of the barn, of Crispus and me; she looks at me, and I remind her of is the witch and my father behind that same plank door. And I look so much like the witch and the rag doll, though no one dares to say it. At least now they can appease God and the priest who always had his eye on me, even when I was a little girl. Maybe he'll bless the sheep and the crops, and they'll fare better than the cattle.

"You are judging me, father, you are judging me, Mother, but your hands are red."

Jak-Ur is at twenty feet. He bellows and grunts, with every pull. One of his legs is useless; he can't even press it against the wall to help; the animals pull him, my whip and my will. But he will soon be up here, facing me.

I do not push fear down the hole;

I face fear with open eyes.

The witch is at the edge of the wood staring at me, as I whip the animals.

I slaughtered a piglet, and the meat is boiling now. I baked spelt bread, and it is still warm. I even found one full wineskin that Ion the Hunter had in his hut. It will be a great feast, Jak-Ur, and I don't care what you do afterward. Strangle me, slaughter me, fuck me. I will not be afraid. Don't throw me down the well, I beg you. But I keep a tiny blade sewn into my dress, you throw me there, and I cut my wrists, and that is it.

Are you judging me, little brother?

Aren't we twins of one womb sheath; don't we share every pain and joy and revenge? Don't you think I wailed when you did? Don't you see that I was raped when you were? Don't you trust me?

It is not enough to kill Jak-Ur, little brother. No, that one I'll keep alive. I have a whole tribe to devour, to bring to their knees. I need his help, his tongue, and his god. I can do it now; I think I know how. The witch did it, she murdered all of us, without ever lifting a knife.

All I have to do is use my mind and their fear. My rage and their god. I am sure they have a god, that tribe, all murderers have one. I'll find him. Trust me, little brother, don't judge me.

Jak-Ur grabs the upper rim of the well with his black fingers. They tremble under his weight; they tremble as he feels the wind and the sun rays, sees the anemones and the chrysanthemums that grow around the well.

You are here, my love. Worship me. Let's feed; feed on each other. They all judge, He does, but who are they? Who gave them the right? I am the only one living. I am the only one with the power to judge.

I slit the priest's throat, but I prayed over his body before I brought you his head:

"And I shall come with arms red, to judge the living and the dead."

Kapoukia

X.
With the Red
Adorning the White

Thirteenth Winter. The Sieve. Eighth Day.

"Black curse. Snow," were the first words that came out of each twelve-wintered mouth on the eighth day. Our luck had run out. The snow came fast in the dark and caught us by surprise, whirling the dance of death. The flakes were flying up and around our heads in the angry wind, not heavily toward the ground. The Reghen had chosen his Story well the previous night when he spoke of the frozen ghosts from the North.

We might have stood until sundown in the rain the days before, but we would last only a few moments under this white cloak of death. I thought they would leave us dressed this time, but the Guides forced us again to take off even our boots.

"They want to kill us all," whispered Atares next to me a little before he fell, defeated, the first to go. He couldn't stand the cold. He couldn't stand the Sieve, even though he knew everything there was to know about it. Maybe *because* he knew everything about it.

The Reghen shouted after a little while, "Any rabbit-heart who can't take the cold, come forward now. Kneel, you cowards, and join the Sheep on an empty belly."

"Hey, you, yellow-liver. Atares is waiting for you." Bako was mocking me. He had seen the agony in my eyes. My bare toes had gone blue in the snow.

Many knelt immediately at the Reghen's words, and before long even more followed. When only eight of us were left, Keko, the cloudy-eyed Guide, approached and threw four pairs of boots, with felt stockings tied to them, like the ones that the great warriors wore. Eight children, four pairs of boots. Instead of boots, some would be picking up their teeth and blood as the snow reddened in front of us.

We had played a game of one word the previous night. Each of us had to make a wish, and the wish could be only one word.

"Meat," said someone.

"Archer," said Matsa.

Malan said nothing.

"Mother," said Elbia.

"Victory," said Bako.

My wish did not fit into one word. Only my curse. But in the snowy field, I now had a one-word wish: "Boots."

I did nothing heroic to help Elbia. Before I even thought of that, Bako brought her down with a hard punch, and Danaka sank her teeth deep into my arm. Danaka still thought I was an easy opponent, meat for the dogs. I hit her repeatedly in the head on that white field, until she lost all consciousness. But she would live. She would lose one toe in the snow, but this would be her pride when she grew up and became an Archer.

"I lost a toe in the Sieve fighting with Malan. And Da-Ren," she would say for winters to come. It was her bravest Story, the one she would greet the Goddess with at the end.

That night, the Guide pulled out Danaka's blackened little toe in one move in the Sheep's tent. I heard many stories of how many children fainted at that sight. "Two children fainted," "three," "all except me"— they all said something different.

Four of us remained who could still walk, one for each pair of boots, when they dragged the rest away quickly so they wouldn't die of cold.

Speechless, with warm feet and bloodied faces, we stood still under the stout gray cauldron of the sky that was pouring white vomit from the belly of the Drakon over our heads. The Drakon of the North, the one place where our ancestors never dared go again.

They didn't let us freeze until the afternoon. It was still early in the morning when the Reghen approached the field again and threw three big pieces of meat, bigger than ever, in front of us. The day's trial had come to an end. Very fast. Almost. Save for one piece.

We all looked at one another for an instant. My whole body stiffened, ready to attack and defend, watching the other three. The wolf was my mother, the Story said. Urak had beaten Bako badly a few breaths before, and I didn't want to roll with him. Malan was as strong as I, and maybe he thought he was stronger. Matsa was definitely weaker, but he was quick. One thing was sure: one of us would starve that day. Malan turned and whispered something to Urak. Urak nodded.

There were never any rules in our fights. Kicks, punches, scratches, stones. Urak attacked Matsa, Malan shrugged his shoulders as if he didn't care to fight, and a breath later he moved fast to punch me. Soon we were wrestling in the white powder. I was stronger than him but didn't want to crush his head. The fight was not ending. He whispered to me as I was holding him back from biting me.

"Let's finish this, Da-Ren. It's Matsa or you."

It was simple. Unjust, I could say now, knowing what the word means, but simple.

All three of us fell on Matsa, and after a few kicks, which we made sure were far from his head, he fell, helpless, at our feet. I ran to the Wolves' tent and began to rub my hands furiously near the fire. Then I roasted my meat, which had become as hard as ice. We three devoured the day's trophy. Matsa's one eye was swollen shut, but with the other, he looked at the meat. I extended my hand to give him some. He deserved it. He tried to take the whole piece. I kicked him hard. If he deserved it, he should have won it himself.

It was still midmorning when we finished eating. We were trapped in the tent with nothing to do, trying to avoid Matsa who stared at me like a one-eyed toothless wolf cub.

Matsa waited for Malan to turn his back and fell on him punching with both fists. Urak joined the brawl, kicking Matsa again. If they let us, we would keep on it all day, fighting the boredom away, isolated in that tent. The Guides felt sorry for us and let us go back outside, warmed and dressed this time, to carry more horse dung. *Felt sorry*—stupid words I come up with, as if I knew what others felt. They probably needed more dung for the fire. It was damn cold.

The marks on the snow, red and brown lines, were fading fast but still showed the way to the Sheep's tents. The four of us played our hearts out. Even Matsa. We rolled around in the snow and had blade fights with wooden poles. As evening fell, I was parrying with Malan when I saw shadows standing out in the pale mist on top of the eastern shed.

I froze. My stick did not rise to block Malan's.

They were standing there. I saw them just for a breath before Malan's stick crashed onto my head. My back hit the ground hard. Matsa and Malan knelt next to me.

"What are you doing?" Malan asked.

Urak was circling around us like a trapped boar.

"Let's get out of here. It's getting dark," he mumbled.

"What happened, Da-Ren?" Malan asked again.

"I saw them, there, on top of the shed. Two Wolfmen standing on two legs. Heads and body of a wolf. And tails. Black fur. I saw them."

"I don't see anyone."

"I saw them, Malan, just for one breath, but they had tails. Wolfmen. Not men."

"Wolf or men, none of us saw them. That stick hit you hard."

Urak was trembling but not saying a word. He had seen them too.

I counted my fingers from the first night of the Sieve, when Selene was less than half. Eight nights had passed. This ninth one coming would reveal her in full, if the Sky's cloudbreaths parted. But the Sky refused.

I got off the snow, leaving behind a few blood marks where Malan had hit me. The children's harmless play ended on that eighth day. The ninth night came dark, its only color the red adorning the white under my torchlight. The Sieve was now ready to dawn on us, razortoothed and merciless.

XI.
Much Worse

Thirteenth Winter. The Sieve. Thirteenth Day.

The mud and the snow fought for the next few days over who would color the field. Our feet prayed. The mud listened. The snow was defeated and round holes of brown earth started to show. The white melted into a net of faint lines that looked like enormous honeycombs. The rain I had cursed the first night returned now as a gift and thawed the earth.

The Guides came and went, taking as few slow steps as possible. They never again touched a cup or a pot, clothing or fire; we did all the work now. Not me, though. Every day three of those who had fallen the day before didn't come to the field. Instead they were assigned the upkeep of our small camp. We called them Carriers. We also started to wake up a little later, not in the middle of the night.

"We do it for us, so we can sleep, not for you," I heard Keko say in between various curses about our mothers. Keko always found a chance to bring up our mothers. Up until the night I learned I was a ninestar, I had never thought about mine.

The Reghen who visited our tent each night, a different face each time, was the only reminder that a world existed outside our camp. They brought four new kids around the tenth day. I spoke to one of them, who told me that he had been snatched from his tent at night and carried for six days by oxcart to get here. He wasn't from Sirol but from one of our outposts on the southern steppe.

We lost two of the children who had never seen the inside of the Wolves' tent. One morning they just didn't show up in the field. Instead we saw a cart carrying little bodies from the Sheep's tents. They told us the children had died. I believed them. They weren't children who could run away. I believed them because the Ouna-Ma was there when they told us.

Two nights later, the cold came back worse than before. On the morning of the thirteenth day, the scorching horse dung smelled like an old horse had peed inside my nose, but its warmth was the most beautiful gift of the Unending Blue Sky. It wasn't really that blue those days. I was in the Wolves' tent again, without Malan, who had fallen for his second time. I was the only one who'd fallen only once. The strongest.

Elbia was with me and eyes would gather on her like flies on meat— all day and all night. The eyes of the other children, the Guides' eyes, even those of the Ouna-Mas followed her. I may have been the strongest in the Sieve so far, but no one looked at me like that.

I was talking to Elbia less and less. These days she was sought after, and someone always managed to be near her before me. I wasn't going to wait in line to speak to her. One day I'd ride the war horses with her, and that was enough of a promise to endure any cold. I wanted to shout to everyone around, "Why don't you all just leave her alone? Can't you see that she doesn't want to talk to you?"

But she did. Elbia's smile burned like a sacred torch of hope, night and day, in the camp of the Sieve. Why did she have a smile for all those boys, even the Guides?

It wasn't a big camp. It was more like a small cage that could fit the suffering and our misery. I measured it once when a Guide on a galloping horse rode all the way from one end to the other. The horse covered the distance before I could breathe slowly a dozen times. A dozen breaths north to south. About the same west to east; that was all. The field in the middle was half the length of the camp. There was only one gate, at the southeast corner, for horses, carts, Ouna-Mas, and death to enter.

The twenty-first day was approaching, but its ghost had not appeared to warn me. Every day was going a little better than the day before. I looked for the Stories and I slept with the Wolves every night to hear them.

Rouba, the old Guide, encouraged me in his own way. "The Reghen will come again tonight. They'll bring a new Story," he would say.

"I will be there," was my answer.

I didn't fall again, not until the twenty-first day.

Instead of a Story on the thirteenth night, the Reghen said only a few words to us, but they were enough. "You are not here to die. They give you too much meat for that. Not like in the other camps. There are forty and more camps like this one with children your age in the Sieve this winter. Children you haven't seen yet. But this one nests the best."

They were the most beautiful words I had ever heard. Whether it was safety or pride that flooded through me, I can't remember. Those are things I try to remember now in the winter of my life, but I can't. Not the events themselves, because they are engraved with iron and fire, deep bloody grooves inside my mind. It is my mind itself that I try to remember, the first thought I had when I was living those moments. What I felt. It would be a lie to say that I remember.

That was how we came out onto the field on the thirteenth day—with the Reghen's word that we were in no danger and we wouldn't be killed. We were the best pack of all the Sieve's camps of the Tribe.

And as the Reghen finished his words, reassuring and beautiful, death arrived hungrier than ever before.

The first girl, Rido, fell too early. She didn't join us the next morning, or the one after that. For days she had almost split in two from coughing, so I was expecting this to happen. It killed me to hear her every morning. Her curly black hair would straighten and cover half of her back every time the rain poured. The curls would rise back when they dried and bounce like they were alive on their own with each cough. Such a sweet little black-haired lamb fighting with the wolves for so many days. She was the thinnest and the shortest, twelve-wintered but half my size, and I dare say the bravest for having stood for thirteen whole days next to us. We would never again see her in the Sieve.

It wasn't long after that when Atares fell next to me.

"You fell again? Are you sick?" I had asked him the day before.

"I know what I'm doing," he answered.

He didn't know shit.

From the first day, he pretended to know everything, but he had been among the first to fall for the third day in a row. He fell first to his knees, two paces away from my feet, and then facedown. He almost made it look real.

I heard them first. I had forgotten them for days now. I turned and saw them, the gray demon-dogs barking and running toward us. Atares was lying next to me, and the maulers were coming straight for me, straight for him.

My legs froze. I didn't run. He wasn't unconscious. I just yelled, "Run, Atares. Now!"

His eyes were open, his ears already knew. He grabbed my calf and tried to get up, but one of the dogs trapped his forearm in its jaw. The second dog went for his neck. I kicked it at the ribs with my free leg, but it made no difference. The boy's fingers slipped away lifelessly, leaving a trail of mud on my skin, as Rouba lifted me in the air and dragged me back. A scream flew out of Atares's mouth. It lasted a few breaths, but I kept hearing it for many nights to come. Children screaming.

It is only when the dogs rip the meat from the thighs with their razor teeth that I ask myself. *Why would the Goddess ever make us leave this life squealing like pigs and sheep? Wouldn't it be more glorious and fitting to turn into a cloud of stardust and rise high in the sky, our brave ashes dancing around Selene, swallowing her light? Weren't we her beloved Tribe? Why did she open us up like a cauldron of meat and red water? Like animals.*

The maulers were the end of fat-mouthed Atares. They shut him up quickly, and forever. I was splattered in long thin lines and splashes of deep red and I smelled like a carcass for two nights until the rain washed me off.

Everyone's face, stomach, and asshole tightened up for the rest of that day. Atares was dragged away into the mist. Up until then, no one had been killed except Ughi on the first night. If I came out a winner, maybe I'd learn that night from the Reghen's mouth why Atares deserved such a fate. It wasn't hard to win that day. So many children were coughing and falling.

The Voice of the Unending Sky came again in the middle of the night to festoon with words the two fresh deaths. The Reghen was talking to the Ouna-Ma. She whispered to him, and he recited her answers. It looked as if he were having a conversation with himself, repeating loudly to us both his questions and the Ouna-Ma's answers.

"Why did Enaka punish Atares?" asked the Reghen.

Like the wind passing through the hides, the Ouna-Ma whispered into his ear and he shouted her words. "Enaka, who sees everything from above, threw a curse on that devious weasel. He fell first every morning for days now, not out of weakness, but to idle alone all day. No one cheats or quails in the Tribe. Enaka sees. Cowards can hide in the vast forest, demons into the deep sea. But may no one ever dare fool her under the Sun, the Selene, and the stars."

The Reghen wouldn't stop.

"Tell us, Ouna-Ma. Will another one die in this way if they cheat?" asked the Reghen.

Again he answered himself with Ouna-Ma's whispers escaping from his gray hood.

"No, not like that. Much worse."

Grim and frozen were all the faces around me except for the giggling laughter of someone after the phrase *much worse.*

It was Malan.

"What if he had the sickness?" I asked him.

"Didn't you hear what they said?"

"And if…"

I was trying in vain. Atares had helped me the first night, but in the end, it was his own scheming mind that did him in.

"Much worse," the Reghen repeated, louder this time so no one would forget. As if anyone would.

I knew there were many worse ways for someone to die in the Tribe. Crucifixions for the othertribal sorcerers of the Cross, impalements with stake slathered in lard for the deserters and traitors, and flaying for those caught stealing from the Khun. I had seen and smelled these deaths in all their horror in Sirol every summer.

The Ouna-Ma stood near the torch unveiled that night, as we all stared, enchanted, at her snake-egg head and her full black eyes. She had painted tears that shone still on her cheeks. But, that night, a true crystal tear did escape between them.

"Why do you shed tears, Voice of the Sky?" asked the Reghen.

"For Rido," replied the Ouna-Ma, who for the first time opened her mouth in front of us.

She then drew her red veil across her face and left us alone and motherless again. Rarely, very rarely, did people have the chance to hear the true Voice of the Sky and to melt as if they had swallowed flaming coal.

That night, after I closed my eyes, I felt a small hand grabbing my calf and then pulled away. Atares's nails leaving their scratch marks on me. Every night, the same nightmare returned. Until the twenty-first night, when I forgot about him completely.

Children continued to fall and disappear in the days to follow, and all from the same cough. A curse had fallen on the Tribe, and the Guides all covered their faces with hoods. They said the black clouds of smoke we had seen rising from the warriors' tents in the south were the bonfires of our dead. A plague, a terrible sickness had spread across Sirol.

"Darhul spews his evil blight on us," Keko the Guide said as he was warming himself again in our tent.

"And that Keko is his murky-eyed servant," I whispered to Elbia. She smiled and covered her face with her hands for him not to see. We hid beneath our hides, away from the breath of death, of Darhul, of the curse, and of the even viler breath that spewed forth from Keko's rotten mouth.

The fear of the evil sickness ruled over our souls. For a while, I lost count of the days. Until a clear night came and Selene was nowhere to be seen. And that's how I found my count again.

Elbia and I overcame the trial every day and slept in the same tent every night. I was full of life, victory, and strength. It was that night, as we were returning to the Wolves' tent, that I saw Rouba, Keko, and the Reghen talking together outside our tent. And for the first time there were two Ouna-Mas beside them. The image of all of them standing there talking jolted me awake.

"How long have we been here?" I asked Elbia.

"Not even a moon," she said, "too early to start counting." Selene showed her face, a thin crescent at the far corner of the Unending Sky. Elbia looked up at the night sky and counted with her fingers.

But I already knew.

The dawn to come would be the twenty-first day.

Apocrypha VI.
Hunt a Wolf for Me

As the One Mother heard the Legends, Chapter VI

Sleep with me, this first winter. You are a broken man. The prison of that well humbled you. My father said that nothing breaks a warrior faster than being in a cell for too long. Once, when he was a soldier, they threw him in a cell for half a moon and he always talked about it.

They don't make cells of pity, to keep men alive. The silence of the cell shutters a man's soul, and it can never be glued back together. Your hobbled leg doesn't help either. You are born and raised a mounted archer, but now can barely ride, and the mule is not much of a ride.

I thought you were going to take me to them, across the river, north. I thought you'd get me to find my mother and that warlord of yours who led you here on his rose gray stallion. I know my mother is not alive, I pray that she isn't. Jak-Ur told me what happens to othertribers; that's what they call those women they enslave.

"No, no," you shake your head.

You can't go back anymore. Is it the leg, or the disgrace of being imprisoned for so long? You can't go back, and it is better that way.

You eat and sleep, sleep and eat, sometimes you stay silent outside the hut, gazing up the sky. Sometimes you limp in slow circles around the well, afraid to look down. You don't touch me, not yet. It is not because you are noble and caring, but because you are weak and defeated. You need more meat to grow strong. Once we slaughter the spring lambs, your vigor will return, and you'll become hungry for me.

It is summer, and we are sweating against each other. You still have no horse, but now you ride me, you bellow and moan, and I squeal like a little animal, you pull my hair, and my gaze meets your Goddess, you don't have a God but a Goddess, oh that I love about your tribe. I love everything about these moments, I labor all day, carrying the weight, and work the land, only to feel that I am riding a dragon, fly above the forest when you are behind me. Oh, make no mistake, I'll have my revenge, and I'll suck the blood out of your veins. But not yet.

That boy Crispus was so handsome with olive eyes and brown hair, clean and beautiful. He lay down next to me with watery puppy eyes, and he too moved, but I didn't feel anything, some pain, discomfort, he winced, he moaned, and then he embraced me, moaning harder, and then stopped, and I was glad it was over.

Now I let you take me, make me a woman worshiped, make me a woman ravaged. Your fingers pressing the bones and the skin around my waist, the pain and pleasure inside me, the summer heat melting my mind. It is the only moment I forget what you are and what I have become. It is the only moment that the ghosts leave me alone. My father never built a chapel, only a small shrine, I've never been to the God's house. I have never experienced the wonder of the holy liturgy, maybe that's why the Devil stole me, my holy liturgy is you screaming and embracing me when it is all over.

It is autumn, and my belly has started to swell. You go north sometimes, to check on them, you fear they might come again. I made a deal with a southern trader, a ruthless man who comes to buy our grain and sheep, and brings me seeds, tar, and a candle every year.

"You will lie to everyone, say that the murrain took all the living here. Make sure no one comes. I'll sell you sheep and grain at half the coin."

He agreed, and nobody from the south comes here anymore. They are afraid of the plague and the barbarians.

Tell me of your tribe. Tell me of a Goddess named Enaka, of the double-curved bow. Tell me everything, so your daughter will listen. I know it is a girl I carry, I feel it fighting me inside, not fulfilling me.

"We can never go back," you say, everyone shares the common women, there is no man and woman together as a couple as there is under God.

It is hard for you to explain all these things, but I learn every word. Your tongue is simple, for children and beasts—you cannot learn mine, you don't care, or you're not smart enough, but I will learn everything about yours. I can already recite Stories about the Reghen now and about the Archers and the Ouna-Mas. Most of the women of your tribe are brood slaves. But there are powerful witches, the Ouna-Mas, the ones with the long skulls. I'll ask the witch, and she will tell me how I can give birth to a longskull daughter. She is the only one who knows, she must be because she is the only one I see other than the trader and you.

You said the witches control their own fate, you drew me the head of the witch, and I've never seen anything like that. I thought you would draw someone with horns and fangs, but the witch is a longskull monster, hairless yet slender, with woman's breasts.

My breasts are getting fuller; I scream at you when you pull and bite at the nipples.

And there are archer women in your tribe, women who can pull that bow you brought with you and shoot arrows. I've tried, sometimes you let me try, only to laugh as I struggle and fail.

"See this, lift this with two fingers first. Only then you try to shoot the bow."

This is a large block of firewood, and you grab it by a worm's hole, and you lift it up and down with two fingers. It weighs as much as a grown child.

"You don't have to learn the bow, woman. I will hunt for you."

"Hunt for me, Jak-Ur."

You see, Jak-Ur, I don't care to shoot the bow to kill you. I can kill you with song and wine in your sleep a thousand times over. The bow is not power, but I so much want to learn the bow, so you stop laughing at me; so that you respect me.

"Do your witches shoot the bow?"

"No, never. You are either witch or archer. Or a common—"

Fuck "common."

"What if one, One, was a witch and an archer?"

"Can't be."

"What if she was?"

"She would be Goddess, not woman," you say.

Oh, this is good, so very good, I like this tribe of yours. I will rip it apart like a little suckling pig on a long winter night roast. Someday, not yet.

"Are all the Ouna-Mas born longskulls?"

"All, except for the First. All her daughters are."

This is good.

Anastasis.

I am so ready, but now I know that I'll have to wait. It will be long.

Sleep with me, Jak-Ur, and when you wake up, remember more stories to tell me.

Feed from my breast, little one, suck my youth; I am going to change your bandages later; your head is so long and beautiful like a quiver. It was so simple to make you a longskull. I didn't even need evil spells or leaves; I just bandaged the head when the bone is young and soft. Now I wrap it tight every three days with fresh cloth.

It is late summer again, and we hide in the witch's hut. She is not here; she never is when I come with Jak-Ur. Jak-Ur told me that we must hide in the forest. He saw them gathering across the river; it is the time when they raid. He is protecting us from his own tribe—we took the animals and escaped in the forest. A basket of skulls is next to the witch's hearth, where the gourds used to be. I think she separated them from the ashes of the sheepfold after the snow drowned the pyre. One skull is staring at me angry as a judging priest.

Feed from my breast, little one, and don't be afraid of all these horrors. I'll protect you from all of them. Oh, I hate you with all my heart, I didn't know it till I saw you, I felt it, but you are Jak-Ur's daughter, the spitting image. I was a vessel he used; a jar left empty now. A jar filled with rage.

I watch from the wood as the archers come and raid. Their warlord, *Khun* they call him, not king, is first there, and his guards surround him. You were one of his guards you say, a *Rod*. But they would never accept you anymore, not after so long, not with that leg of yours.

I carry the little one with me whenever I go, I carried her since she was so small, almost like a rabbit, a rabbit with your vile eyes, and I have carried her for two winters now. You don't have years; you count winters and moons—I know everything about you, never forgot a word you uttered. I can recite most of the Stories and the Legends. The she-wolves were your mothers?

"Hunt a wolf for me, Jak-Ur. Can you do that for me? Bring me the hide of the wolf, its head."

Good, good. You are trained well now, like that puppy I had.

I carry the little girl with me everywhere. Always did since she was born. I made a hole in a hide and I wrap her in it. I place the two arrow fingers of my right hand in the hole to lift her up and down. She likes the sway; it puts her to sleep. She keeps growing and getting bigger; I still carry her with two fingers.

I can almost stretch the bowstring now. One more winter. Laugh as much as you want, one more spring. Then you will meet your Goddess.

Come the first full moon of spring, I go and light a candle for my little brother. It is the one thing I do all year, the one night I remember the dead when life returns to melt the snow and paint the fields.

Come summer, we hide in the forest to escape the war dogs. The witch is never there when I go with Jak-Ur and for some reason that scares me. She only appears when I come alone.

Jak-Ur wants a son, but I will never give him one. He doesn't deserve one, and I am afraid that I might love my son, that he might look like my brother. I rub my insides with vinegar and resin, and I let you take me, make me scream and laugh wild with pleasure, but I will never give you a son. You pray; pray as much as you like, I am stronger than your Goddess, and she won't listen to you.

Make no mistake; you are here to serve my revenge.

I want to know all your songprayers, Jak-Ur.

"Oh Goddess, sweet and beautiful…"

Oh, don't whimper. Not yet.

XII.
The Twenty-First Day

Thirteenth Winter. The Sieve. Twenty-First Day.

Death could not rest and sent his Redveils. The Ouna-Mas slid into our tent and, after a short while, pointed at me while whispering with the Reghen.

I was sitting with Elbia next to the fire.

"Can I see your mark?" I asked, and she lifted her hair to reveal the lucky sevenstar sign, the black circle behind her ear.

"I will tell you a secret." I spoke to her loudly so that the Guides, the Ouna-Mas, and the Reghen would hear me. "This isn't my twelfth but my thirteenth winter. They had forgotten me at the orphans. How can they know what day I was born when they don't even remember which winter? I was wrongly marked."

My voice had to reach the ears of the Redveils for my luck to change.

"You will be a great warrior, whatever mark you carry. We will ride the war horses together, Da-Ren," Elbia answered.

There was no Story that night. We lay next to each other to sleep. I opened my eyes. She was looking straight at me. I smiled. My fingers meshed with hers, and the fire burnt warmer and deeper than ever. She didn't pull her hand away. Our fingers touched and moved, slowly rubbing together for countless breaths, my heart racing, our eyes closed.

I dreamed of the Endless Forest. It was green and gold.

I awoke in a cold sweat.

I dressed slowly, I ate slowly. I wanted to just stop time. To not face the dawn of the twenty-first day.

"It's time to go out," Rouba said to me when I was the last one left in the tent.

I want to throw up. The words didn't come out.

"It matters not when we will leave this place, Da-Ren. Only that we tell our best Stories when we meet Enaka in the Unending Sky."

With those words, old Rouba led me out of the tent on the longest winter's night. The Reghen told us it was the longest when they woke us at daybreak.

"We won't leave here alive," I said to Elbia as we stepped into the frigid air.

"What's got into you? Stop searching for your ruin, and it will not find you," she said, her voice angry for the first time.

I was not the one searching. Death was upon us, stealing the children away, his night fires spread across Sirol to consume the corpses. If it wasn't the maulers, it was the plague, or the ninestar curse, the heads of Darhul, there were nine of them too, and the thousand teeth of the Drakon. It was always something.

When we arrived at the field, everyone knew that this day would be different. Elbia swallowed hard when she saw the Archers riding, the hooves raising a cloud of dust that blended with the morning mist.

Standing in front of the warriors were five Reghen and several Ouna-Mas. More than ten, standing in their robes like a black forest of firs.

Six massive men on foot surrounded the strongest horse I had ever seen and were holding the banners of Khun, the One Leader of the Tribe. They wore dark-brown bearskins and had a red cloth tied around each arm. Bako all excited and smiling, shouted, "Rods." His mouth continued to gape. It was the Khun's guards, the tallest men of the Tribe, and that meant that the man on the whitest of horses was none other than Khun-Taa.

"The Khun always comes on the last day. We will leave here. Today even," Elbia told me.

She was right. Almost.

I could swim forever in her smile. I had learned to swim in the marshy waters of Blackvein where Ughi's body was still floating.

We children stood in one line, fully dressed this time. The weakest pale sun to ever rise upon Sirol broke over the horizon. He too looked as if he had fallen from the plague and the Goddess had covered him in white goatskins to heal him. So faint and small that if I blew he would go out.

Sah-Ouna separated herself from the others, and walked to a cut tree trunk that stood twenty paces in front of me. A sacred knife was in her hand, not a fighting blade, but the one with a black-horned handle. She waited.

"Sacrifice," Atares whispered next to me. I turned to find his face. There was no one there. Atares had been torn to pieces by the dogs just days before. What demon stole his voice?

Sacrifice. He was right. The black-horned knife, Sah-Ouna, all the others. Sacrifice. Those watching formed a circle around the field, and in the center stood the children, six times the fingers on my one hand, many. The Reghen with their gray robes and the greatest warriors, those with the whitest of horses, were on the north side her stares fixed on the First Witch. The Ouna-Mas were murmuring a solemn song, one of them ululating and piercing my head.

I was boiling in a giant cauldron of agony with Elbia at my side. I wanted her next to me that day. Maybe some of her sevenstar luck would rub off on me. To my surprise, Keko didn't separate us. He knew.

Her fingers touched mine again.

"All of them came here for me," I whispered to her.

She squeezed my hand. Tiny silver moons shone in her eyes. We always try to guess. What the eyes say, the stars, the Goddess's signs. But we never learn.

The stars and the wind remained silent, as if they had run out of Stories to warn me. I had tried to cough for days and nights to see if I had the sickness, but I didn't. I was as strong as I had ever been, even stronger than before the Sieve, when I'd rarely even seen meat. It was a cruel fate, but I would die stronger than ever. It was too late to escape. I would just make a fool of myself if I tried to run now, in front of everyone, while the Goddess watched. She would feed me to Darhul herself. Elbia watched. I wouldn't run.

A Guide approached Sah-Ouna, carrying a bleating black ram behind his neck, its front legs on the right side of his shoulder and its hind legs over the left. He lowered it, tied two ravendark ribbons around its horns and held it on the tree trunk in front of the First Witch.

I exhaled my whole life. The tree trunk was there for another soul, one as black-fated as mine. I was not the sacrifice.

Warriors passed; one threw barley and others poured milk onto the tree trunk.

Sah-Ouna raised her hand and the song of the Ouna-Mas died. The First Witch spoke: "Goddess, accept this offering from us and take away the sickness. Do not ask for any more lives from your Tribe, and we will give you this blood, the purest that we can offer."

She stepped next to the tree trunk where the Guide was holding the ram down flat. Its desperate bleating was the only sound, as if it disagreed with its fate. With one steady and slow movement Sah-Ouna opened the animal's throat. Blood flowed, first onto her hands and then onto the wood. She emptied the life of the ram into a bowl, then tore the animal's belly in half and offered the heart to the Sky. She moved her lips in silence for a few breaths and returned the heart to the wood. She took out the liver, raised it, examined it briefly in the pale-yellow light of the sick sun, and then turned her head toward Khun-Taa.

She shook her head negatively.

Two Rods left their guard beside the Khun and approached Sah-Ouna. She turned, and her gaze fell directly on me.

"She's coming," I whispered to Elbia, who had glued herself next to me. The Rods were following her.

I would never know why. That hurt the most. What difference did it make if I had been born nine or eight days after the full moon? Wasn't I the best in the Sieve? With bloodied hands and a slow step, Sah-Ouna kept walking toward me. The sun was high on the horizon, but even the birds remained mute. Not even the whinnying of a horse broke the frozen silence. The only sound was the mud squelching beneath her feet on every step.

Sah-Ouna was one step away from me.

What was the darkness in her eyes? Sorrow, duty, sacrifice, a Goddess's demand?

The Demon always looks you in the eye. I knew the Legend.

Sah-Ouna stopped, dipped her hand into the bowl, lifted it, and with her arrow finger painted, slowly, mercilessly, a red circle. On the woolen tunic, high above the chest. Elbia's chest.

The Witch and the Rods moved to the sides. Across from us stood seven warriors with their heads down. Seven, yes, I'm pretty sure of it.

Elbia turned to look at me with intense, wide-open eyes. Bright eyes swallowing life and the whole world in one breath.

"Da-Ren. What? I…"

A drop ran down her cheek. It wasn't raining.

It happened before I took another breath. I never had a chance to think, to step forward. My eyes were fixed at hers, not at the men opposite. A mesmerizing whistling song ripped the air and, like a deer entranced, I turned to find it. So fast. The seven arrows pierced the thin white fabric that covered Elbia's young breasts.

She never had time to say a word. She fell next to me with eyes still wide-open. All seven had found the red circle. And they formed seven red smaller circles. Full circles. Like seven stars.

Did I count them? No. I didn't have time. But there must have been seven. All acts of the Goddess and the Witches had meaning. There couldn't have been six or even eight. I think. I didn't count. It was all so fast.

It was then that Enaka's icy tongue slid into my ear and carved an eternal memory in my mind. Children screaming. Were they screaming for Elbia? Or for the quivers still full of arrows?

The Guides charged toward us. Children's bodies slammed into one another and in the pandemonium someone knocked me down. Before I got up a knee hit me hard in the head. Children, Guides, Archers all running around me. Whips waving in the air. I tried to crawl to Elbia's body, to twine our fingers again, one more time, but the Guides had already taken her away.

The warriors lowered their bows, the Guides fell back, the children stopped screaming. The Witch had already turned her back. There would be no more sacrifices. Only the best of the Sieve. I wasn't the best after all. I wasn't the one torch of glowing hope every night among the rest.

The strangest thing happened that morning. At the exact moment I knew I wasn't going to die from my mark, I was marked by death forever. Those arrows marked me so that I now believed I did carry a curse. I would bring darkness and blood to the Tribe. One day, I would.

I crept into the Sheep's tent uninvited and stayed there curled and trembling till dusk.

Her face clean, her body dressed and adorned as a warrior Archer, Elbia lay upon a wooden bed in the twilight of the twenty-first day. Everybody took a twig to throw into the pyre, to become accomplices, and beneficiaries. "Sacrifice," Atares had said that fateful morning.

Danaka gave me a twig as well. She tried to hold my hand. I pulled it away. The warriors came too and in a rare show of respect, dismounted from the horses. Sah-Ouna was holding the pine torch, the firestarter. She raised her hands to the Unending Sky and cried out, ripping the life out of my chest. "Enaka, take the plague of the Drakonsnakes away from us, as you take this one up to the stars. We offer you our bravest soul, the one who faced all deaths."

Elbia, daughter of Enaka. That was what I called her from the first time I saw her riding. I want to see my mother again, she said. War horses, she said.

The sun set in a blaze of vibrant color, stronger and well fed, when our brown twigs and Elbia's brown hair went up in flames. He laid himself triumphantly to sleep in the west, his body full of the day's blood.

I fell to my knees, and my hands covered my face. My chest heaved in spasms. I bit my lips to control myself. And then I broke down. I did not shed a furtive tear or two. I cried with a wailing that shattered my whole body and with burning poison water that I could no longer hold in. I cried on my knees in front of Khun-Taa and Sah-Ouna, the fierce warriors and the rest of the children.

Another Guide whom I had not seen before, grabbed me, like the first night, by the hair and dragged me away from the funeral pyre. He tied me to the stake where they had nailed the ram's head, away from everyone else. Only the stars and Elbia watched, as he lashed me seven times like a dog. To this day, I can remember those seven lashes.

The first one felt like I was being torn by the teeth of a thousand dogs. The second burned me like the flaming tongues lit by Sah-Ouna. With the third, I begged silently for it to be the last even if it meant death. The fourth ripped the skin so deeply that I could feel the leather and the nails on my liver. The fifth was sweet because it brought me closer to the end and to Elbia. The sixth, dishonorable, marked me on my forehead and my left temple, and the seventh—I barely remember the seventh, but there must have been a seventh.

The whip's serpents of shame, engraved on my back, healed as I grew older, but the scars on my face stayed for life.

Some scars mark us forever.

Ouna-Ma Longskull

XIII.
Baagh, Baaghushai

Island of the Holy Monastery, Thirty-Second Summer.
According to the Monk Eusebius.

"Young man. Sorcerer of the Cross. Save us!" begged the barbarian offering the jar he had just carried for thirty-eight and a thousand steps.

The white pigeons that were carelessly nibbling in the monastery's courtyard fluttered like frightened wind spirits and flew high to the battlements. The chickens could not follow and made best by scurrying away as far as they could. The Castlemonastery had impenetrable walls, stone-built and tall as six men, to deter all invaders. Except for the woodworm, which had slowly devoured the main cedar gate. On that quiet day, none of us had managed to secure it at first sight of the small merchant vessel. The invader was already within us.

When they heard my cries, about a dozen monks ran as fast as their brown robes would permit to take the place of the pigeons in the courtyard. The First Elder was at the front, holding his arms wide open to keep the rest back. White-bearded and of sturdy build, fearless in front of any danger that this earthly world harbored, the First Elder commanded the man, "In the name of God, leave your blades outside this holy place and repent, barbarian. What do you seek? Are you of the faith? The Son of God prevails."

Da-Ren showed that he did not understand so many words, so fast, and began to panic. He turned his sweat-drenched head left and right, and his eyes darted from one face to another as if he were desperately looking for someone.

"I've brought my offering," he said, holding out the jar again, and the First Elder motioned for me to take it. But the man would not let it go.

"Baagh. Baaghushai!" he yelled.

He repeated the words many times. The monks, perplexed, whispered to one another, each trying to recognize the strange words, but in vain. As Da-Ren's strength began to fail him, the *ai* at the end of the unintelligible word began to fade. And then I understood—as if I were sent by God Himself to be the only one who could understand this man, and the words leaped out of my youthful soul. "Baaghushai. Baaghus. Baaghus. He is looking for the monk Evagus."

His eyebrows lifted, and the wrinkles on his forehead deepened as his head nodded with excitement.

"Baaghus, Baaghus. Baagh."

"Evagus has isolated himself for days now at the hermitage in the northern cave," the monk Rufinus said in a low voice next to the First Elder.

Evagus the hermit, the secretive, the traveler. He had come to the Castlemonastery on an imperial naval trireme from the north only a few days before Da-Ren. The First Elder and the older monks welcomed him like an old friend. They knew him from the days of his youth, when he first arrived to receive the rites of the True Faith, when he still called himself Baagh. He had once been a pagan wizard from the east. He trained and cultivated his faith in the searing deserts of the south and the east, some said as far away as the cursed city of Varazam.

A few of the suspicious monks whispered that he may still be worshipping a different, false god on some faraway land. On different occasions, I witnessed the First Elder doubting or exalting Evagus, whichever of the two suited him at the time. But the official story among us was that Evagus had chosen for years now the faith of our one true God.

When he arrived on Hieros Island, he told us to call him Evagus and demonstrated that he was undoubtedly a man of the Faith. And of power. He carried a gold-sealed edict from the Emperor himself, who asked that we host and help him as he required, but even the Emperor's gold seal had no power in the Castlemonastery. Only the First Elder had jurisdiction there.

"Baaghus, Baaghus, yes, he is here," I answered the barbarian.

"Be calm now, he will come. We will go and summon him. Give me your blades," the First Elder commanded, but to no avail.

Da-Ren, half crawling, as if he had lost all strength upon entering sacred ground, crouched into the only corner within the courtyard that was sheltered from the noonday sun. The way he still held the jar, I was certain it was filled with gold and gems—but that was far from the truth.

His tall body rocked with spasms, the two scabbards marking his back like the Cross of the Martyr. As he was sitting there with his back turned, it would have been so easy to hit him over the head with a heavy piece of wood, if we could find the wood and the courage. But no monk could do that, even if this man was likely to bring death to us all.

I was sent immediately to the remote hermitage to bring Evagus back to the monastery. The one they called Baaghus or Baaghushai or Baagh. From this point, I will refer to him as Baagh since papyrus costs a lot to buy from traders. That's the name Da-Ren used.

Spring had covered the paths with thorny bushes and thick weeds, and it took me longer than expected to reach Baagh. I found him sitting in the cave with his head bowed. He lifted it only when he heard the rolling pebbles shifting beneath my sandals, unintentionally heralding my arrival.

He ignored me as if I were invisible, so I was forced to shout. "Evagus! We beseech you. It is a matter of life and death. A sword-bearing barbarian has arrived. He is a man from the distant north, judging from his clothes. He has a mark on his face."

"On the left side."

"I think so."

"Earlier than I thought. Did he ask for me?" His words came out hoarse, as he likely hadn't spoken for many days.

"Yes. Well, he asked for someone called Baaghushai."

Baagh was on the move, and I was following.

"Does he have a large cut on his left arm?" he asked.

"Yes. And many smaller marks all over his face. He's holding a jar."

"A gray jar with a red circle?"

"No, a green and black one."

"Strange."

We were already outside the cave walking fast. I called out to him that I had brought water and an apple to give his legs strength for the walk back. He had been alone at the northern cape night and day with little water and, according to the Canon, he would eat a small piece of bread with salt once a day for a week. He took the water flask and a bite of the apple.

The only way for any traveler or invader to reach the Castlemonastery, or even the rest of the island, from the sea was to climb the thirty-eight and a thousand steps. The steps ascended straight out of the sea like a slithering monster sent from Hell to devour the few believers who were seeking refuge behind our walls.

The monastery itself was called a castle because it was the only passage through which travelers could reach the rest of the island. Its walls protected the monks, and the peasants, from pirates and invaders. There was only one small hidden harbor, its only dock on the eastern side. The harbor's mouth was at the southeast corner, visible only to those who approached from the south just before they were about to crash onto the southern cliffs. That harbor led to the steps that Da-Ren had climbed.

The other sides of the island all ended in steep cliffs. No one other than the island's wild goats could climb them. The whole island had been created by God to be a natural fortress, immovable and impenetrable, an ideal place for many other defenseless monasteries to hide their gold.

The church separated the yard into halves—one for the peasants, one for the monks—both reaching the main gate. The monks and the peasants would meet at the gate or at the church but never in the monks' yard. There were many sinuous paths from the Castlemonastery leading to the rest of the island. They passed through the huts and the sun-baked crops of the villagers and led all the way to the northern and western cliffs.

We took one of those paths, wedged between thorns and sage bushes. Their flowers, the color of purple mourning, reminded me of the mortal danger that had landed on the shores of Hieros Island.

Baagh's aged face flushed red and dripping with sweat as he straddled the knee-high xerolithos fences. He was moving as fast as he could, shouting, "Run! We won't make it in time."

We returned to the Castlemonastery faster than it had taken me to reach him.

As unbelievable as it seemed to me, these two men from two opposite sides of the world greeted each other like brothers.

"He has been lying cuddled like that since you left," Rufinus said.

Baagh ran, embraced the man and held his head to his chest, speaking softly to him. Then he turned and announced to all of us: "Be at ease, brothers. This is Da-Ren, a disciple of mine. He means no harm to any of you."

Of all the monks of our monastery, Baagh had a unique gift that I learned of later: he could shout out lies as easily as he could the truth. That barbarian was no disciple. A gray-white pigeon seemed to believe him, though, and returned to the courtyard close to his feet. The rest remained perched like marble statuettes on the bell tower as if they knew better. Baagh whispered, only to me, to bring a wooden cup of hot water and to throw in a handful of sleepflower and another of valeriana.

"Throw in *what*? That will bring down an ox."

"Bring it before it's too late."

"We don't have enough valeriana."

"Throw in all that we have. All of it. And tell someone to hurry up and bring the blacksmith from the village to chain him as soon as he falls asleep."

"Is he dangerous?"

"He can massacre the whole island with one arm tied. He is the most dangerous man that I have met on the four corners of this Earth," Baagh said, just as the other monks were starting to approach.

"He is the Devil disguised," the monk Rufinus murmured behind me, moving his three fingers here and there.

"Almost. He is Da-Ren," said Baagh. "The Devil has been trying to do away with him since he was a child."

The man slowly rose to his feet from his corner as if he were just emerging from a demonic possession and calmly looked Baagh in the eye. "I don't have time. I brought the offering, Baagh. I did everything you told me. You must help me. Now!"

Baagh went closer and whispered barbaric words to him while caressing the back of his neck with the palm of his hand. He gave him the cup I brought and implored him to drink all of it. The man looked at the faces around him for a few instants and in between sips exchanged a few more unintelligible words with Baagh. He grew more lethargic with every sip. After a while, he leaned back into his corner but face down this time, unconscious and heavy as a corpse. I untied with great effort the scabbards and the belt that were strapped tightly around his body to remove his blades.

Two monks, the blacksmith, and I carried his heavy body down the dark rock steps and laid him down in the underground prison. My bones suffered from the pain, but I endured without complaint as I did throughout every ordeal.

We passed the double-bolted cells where we kept the olive oil, wheat, and other offerings and valuable gifts from the devout, and reached the far end of the cellar. There, where no one ever went unless something terrible had happened. All in all, there were three dark cells. One for the lepers, which thankfully had been locked and empty for years now, one for isolation and repentance for great sin, and the third that housed the bones of our departed holy brothers. This third one was the brightest of all when the sun rays made it through the narrow window and reflected off the rain-washed bones. But there was no light to be seen in those hollow eye sockets, saintly as they were.

We put him in the second one, since we had no cells for prisoners in the monastery. Not until then.

"Quick, the chains!" cried Baagh.

The blacksmith had only one chain with one ring that we placed on his ankle and nailed it to the ground with an iron awl. If he were as strong as he looked, he would be able to loosen the awl but not break the chain. I had never before seen us treat another human being in this manner in this holy place, as if he were a rabid infidel dog and we his tormentors in Hell.

I was taught to forsake deceit and violence and to use prayer to tame the tortured souls who visited us. Baagh warned us to act differently with this man. I despaired at the thought of his demise and couldn't help but cry for him as if he were my own brother.

When the blacksmith's hammer fell heavier than usual and the sound echoed against the naked and damp stone walls, the barbarian murmured deliriously his own mysterious words.

"Zeria…Varazam—"

"Thankfully, he hasn't slept for days. He feared that the ship wouldn't stop at the island. He told me that he barely shut his eyes for many days," Baagh said.

We left him like that, senseless and chained, across from a small window without shutters that looked out onto an abysmal precipice, this being his only evidence of the outside world, of time, of the sun.

Forty days passed before I saw the chained man again. My life had gone back to its daily routine, and only a fleeting thought, like the spur of Satan, would creep into my mind at night. I would be seized by a secret longing to dip my finger into the honey again. But Baagh took away the jar that Da-Ren brought. When I asked him about it, he told me, "I buried it."

I didn't believe him.

The First Elder reminded me to remove the image and the sin of the infidel from my mind and to return to my fast of mouth and thought.

Only Baagh would take food to him for the first month. In that time, in the name of the heavenly Father and with the fear of his infernal adversary, who may just have been the inmate of our prison, Baagh persuaded the monks to allow the man to live. He used the imperial edict as leverage when they at first suggested to starve him to death.

The Castlemonastery was a small nest built to house fifty souls at the tip of a rock. The walls protected most of the eastern and southern sides. The northern and western sides were protected by the mountain rock rising like a heavy gray curtain. The sun set early at the monastery, having the huge rock on its western back. At the far end of the monastery, perched high on the rock, was the monks' two-story building, the rooms of the second floor and the refectory. Each narrow window of each small cell praised the sun that rose above the sea every morning. The dungeons extended underneath the whole yard. The supplies and heirloom cellars were under the monks' building because we wanted them close by. The three cells, those of Da-Ren, the lepers, and the skeletons were all the way across at the northeast corner. Each one had a small window opening toward the cliff.

Baagh took me with him the night he went to free Da-Ren, with the other monks' consent. When we entered the dungeon, the summer moon was too small to provide us with enough light in the middle of the night. We brought the oil lamps close to his face. He looked even more terrifying lying there, grimy and trapped, stirring on all fours like an animal. Da-Ren saw me and turned his back to me curled up like a worm that wanted to hide in the smallest crack in the corner. I was startled and took a step back when I saw the chain loose and unhinged from the floor and the dry blood around his ankle. It would be so easy for him to strangle and kill us right there with that chain.

"Be careful!" I yelled to Baagh, but he reassured me.

"He won't hurt you. Don't be afraid."

Baagh turned toward Da-Ren as if he was simply continuing a conversation that had been left unfinished. "You must listen to me and be patient, Da-Ren. The monks here at the Castlemonastery do not possess the magical powers that you seek. I will need time to travel to find the ones who hold the secret and bring them back."

"You had told me, Baagh, that here in this place I would find the all-powerful Sorcerers of the Cross. Those who had the power to command life and death. You are my last hope to save them," Da-Ren said without turning around.

Baagh unlocked the chain from Da-Ren's leg and left a clean white cloth with a bowl of fresh water next to him. I took a few steps back until my hands stopped on the slimy wall.

"I will tell you, Da-Ren, what I am going to do. Turn and look at me," Baagh said.

We waited there for a while until Da-Ren turned around.

"Da-Ren, I took off your chains for good. Tomorrow you will move to one of the cells where we host our visitors. Eusebius will come to see you every day."

Baagh looked at me. I swallowed hard. What trials the Lord had brought onto me. The old man continued.

"He will read to you from the books and the scriptures until you both fall tired every day, and he will tell you stories and teach you to speak our language properly. He is a kind young man and harbors no hate or rage within him. He came here an orphan. When you are ready, I want you to tell him your story."

"No."

"Listen to me. This is the island of God and if you want his help, you will do His will. When you begin, then and only then will I set sail to find the almighty monks, the Anchorites of the desert of the east and south. Those who have the power to help you."

"What are you talking about? There is no time for that," answered Da-Ren, with his trembling hands shaking an imaginary neck that he wanted to strangle. This empty cell was torture for someone like him, who had lived his life as a warrior. He needed an enemy and a blade.

"From the beginning. You will tell Eusebius everything, Da-Ren. Only I know what you are, but all the other monks must learn as well if they are to help you. Eusebius…" Baagh turned toward me. "When Da-Ren is ready to speak to you, you will transcribe the story of his life on papyrus."

"Me?"

My surprise triumphed over shame and became desire. I wanted to do this. This challenge brought a feeling of sweet and irresistible impatience. The six psalms and the true hymns could not compare to this. Baagh continued, "I will supply you with all the materials you need: papyri, ink of two colors and reed pens, and anything else you want. Fortunately, he has brought gold with him and so have I. We have enough for you to begin, and you will be able to order more from the merchant ships."

Da-Ren then turned around and grabbed his chains with both hands as if he wanted to free himself from an even worse evil hovering over him.

"I don't have…don't have time, Baagh. The demons ravage the Blackvein. Death. Zeria. Aneria. I must save them. Magus of the South. Why do you torture me? I twice saved your life."

"And I yours, many times over. And that is what I want to do now. You will learn our words."

"I already know them."

"Not well enough. You will learn them better, and you will tell Eusebius your entire story. With every detail. Do you hear me? With every detail, or else you will never see me again. You finally have to rid yourself of this curse you have carried with you since birth."

I put an end to the whistling of a mosquito on my cheek with the palm of my hand so that I could better hear the fate that Baagh had chosen for me.

"The monastery will offer you peace, Da-Ren. In return, it asks for your cooperation and service. And your repentance if you choose, of course. I will bring the powerful Sorcerers of the Cross. In exchange, I ask for your story."

"Let me go now, Baagh. Let me go back."

"That is not possible, Da-Ren. There is no return. You know that. No ship will offer you passage, and you will never cross the sea straits of the Holy Empire on your own. They are at war again. When they see you, they will immediately know what you are."

With those words, Baagh motioned to me that it was time for us to leave.

"I cannot understand why you are asking this of me, monk Evagus," I said as soon as we walked out of the man's cell.

"But you will understand when you finish."

"Which Holy Apostle shall I begin with? Shall I read to him the Five Holy Books, the new Canon, or the Aphorisms of the First Elder?" I asked. "I have recently written them down."

"Do you know children's tales? Folk stories of the peasants of the island? You can start with those, with the simplest ones. Teach him the words for the flowers and the trees. But listen carefully. You will teach him only the words for the essential things, the nouns. For only knowledge of the nouns paints the world of God. The verbs, most of them are the hole-filled vessels of Satan. Adjudicate. Condemn.

Command. Judge. Criticize. All these verbs are not righteous work for the pious. Leave them alone, for only God should use them in a story of your fellow man."

I had so many questions, most of which I didn't yet know I had.

"Always use the abbreviated code of the sacred writing, Eusebius. Whoever reads it should know that it is the work of God-fearing people."

"Is what I am about to transcribe a holy story?"

"Exactly the opposite," said Baagh, as he abandoned me at the blade-carved gate of a thousand-day labyrinth.

Apocrypha VII.
It is Time, Jak-Ur

As the One Mother heard the Legends, Chapter VII

The truth is I never loved you. You came uninvited, you ravaged my body and sucked out my youth. You didn't bring anything good with you, and I could never even stand your face. Your piggy eyes narrow and dark, looking even darker when you tried to smile. A barbarian scum of the steppe, that's all you are, you never belonged here. You've been here what, close to seven years now, and I say that is enough. You never called me "mother." This is not a word the tribe uses, and we never taught you the word. You call me "Sarah" as he does, yet you call him "father."

It will make things easier tomorrow.

"Come here, girl, don't go close to that well. How am I ever going to get you out of there, if you fall?"

"What is down there, Sarah?"

"Darkness my child, darkness staring up at you."

"I am afraid, Sarah."

"Don't be, child. Not yet."

It seems so terrible, yet it is not. It is the fate of us all, and you will have to find yours earlier because your fate defines mine. I need you; I need your death. Not only to crush him, I need it to fulfill my destiny. You will not suffer any of the miseries all other women do. It is the first full moon of spring tomorrow. At dawn, I'll light the candle for my little brother as I do every year, my child.

Jak-Ur came looking worried yesterday, running to me; he didn't even bring the kill from his hunt.

"They are crossing the river," he said. "We need to hide in the forest."

"Why? This early in spring?"

"I saw Reghen and Ouna-Mas crossing. They are coming to worship the spring, to climb the hill and pray. They are preparing for a big campaign. Too many horses and carts gather by the north bank, ready to cross. This summer they may raid Sapul."

Their Sapul is our Holy Thalassopolis, the Empire's reigning city.

"The Khun?"

"Yes, Khun-Taa has crossed south, he leads thousands of them. It is time."

"It is time, it is time, Jak-Ur," I repeat.

We don't have to hide in the forest, child; not this time. I've been hiding in there each summer for seven years; I never see the witch anymore, rowan trees have grown and surrounded her hut; they must be seven-year-old trees. Their bleeding berries grow in autumn when we abandon the forest to return to the fields. I am afraid of the rowan, I am afraid of that one truth, that the witch is never there when I go with you and Jak-Ur.

I had an evil dream the other night; we were dancing in a circle, the witch, the rag doll, and me, all three of us looking so much alike. We kept swirling and dancing faster and faster, and the wolves gathered and howled around us and the fire. We were moving so quickly that I felt my body and my soul pass through that of the witch and the rag doll. So fast round and round; all three of us became one, and I was now flying, gliding above the leaves. I had no toes, and my laughter was a scream. I could taste the hatred of the witch for my father; I could taste the chicken blood on the lips of the rag doll. Mother spat at me. Can it be? Can it be that there was never a witch or a rag doll? Was I the witch all along? No, that can't be, that would mean that father, the barn, leading the war dogs to our village, knowing and hiding, no, this is just my mind tormenting me, it can't be. Not that it matters anymore because come tomorrow, I will become the witch. I just can't believe that I was the witch all along, the death of them all, no that is just an evil nightmare, and I will not believe it. It doesn't matter anymore, though, because I already doubt my mind and my life, who I was, and who they were. It is a terrible thing to lose your mind, for truth, nightmare and legend to mix into one. But that terrible thing will help me, come tomorrow.

There are a few things I am still certain of. I had a dog, a puppy. I remember that I buried it many years ago. I unearthed it the other night, only to make sure that I am not losing my mind. Only frail bones left; the molosser broke its front leg. I am certain that I had a little brother, I carried eight sacks with his remains, and I had to empty the sack each time because I didn't have eight sacks to spare.

I know for sure that I have a man named Jak-Ur and a seven-year-old girl. I boiled our fattest hen, and I'll bake fresh bread for the feast of spring tomorrow. And I'll boil the sleepflower, and the mushroom of the forest, the one that brings eternal peace. We will gather around the fire for the last time after the sun sets.

Drink, my child, drink and forget, rest your head, rest your long quiver head next to your father's, let me lull you into the darkness, the songprayer of the tribe, the song of Enaka.

O Goddess, sweet and beautiful,
come listen …
the woman mourns her offspring.
…
The darkness cries the sorrow's song,
…And I will bring as sacrifice,
a young heart of my own blood.

I skip the words so that you can sleep faster. What a beautiful song that is, the one you always favored.

Sleep now, the eternal sleep, but don't worry, I'll keep you with me forever.

You, now. Once again it is time, Jak-Ur. Didn't I tell you that I'll kill you with song and wine? You have mocked me for so long, but now that the sleepflower takes you and your arms and legs fail you, what are you going to do? You are not a small girl, and this will not kill you, but do not mock me again. I am strong now, and I can even pull your bowstring. I can carry you out of the longhouse, to the field, upon the wheelbarrow and take you all the way to the well. The fall will wake you;

the crush will probably kill you this time if you are lucky. You are half awake but can't move your limbs; you barely open your mouth to mumble my name.

"Sarah, Sarah."

Even uttering my name is hard in your stupor.

Down the well, you fall once more, and now you know that I was the one who threw you down years ago, the one who made you a cripple and an exile.

It is a full spring moon, and I see you once again down there, but this is the last time. No meat and no water anymore, no daughter, your offspring is sleeping on my arms the eternal sleep before I rest her in the pyre. Look at me and scream in despair, hear my words, no need for hand signs anymore, I know your tongue so hear me now:

"You savage beasts murdered everyone I loved, everyone I cared about. It is your nature, and I can accept it, but you, Jak-Ur should have never touched my brother. Shhh, don't talk, don't try, I haven't gone mad, you should know that I planned it all along; my revenge will not be complete if you don't understand that I planned it all along, that you never had me, and every time I gave myself to you was for the pleasure of this moment. This is true slavery and rape, Jak-Ur, to let someone so much inside you that when she betrays you, she rips apart every limb and joint of yours. The pain, feel it. Do you still think you got inside me all those times? No, I got inside you, only to break you apart now; I raped you.

"I had a dog once, I had a brother, I had a man, and a daughter. You can't scream, only mumble 'Sarah, Sarah,' and even that is hard for you. Now you can weep because this is the end, the end of you and your offspring. It is only my beginning. I will find your tribe, I will find your Khun, and I will avenge my brother. You are exiled to the darkness forever, you'll die of thirst, hunger, and sorrow down there, as it should have happened all along. You will see a soft glare covering everything soon, but it is not your Goddess descending. I am building a pyre, for her body. I'll rest the bones of our only child in there. Beg, as my brother begged, mumble your dying grief: 'Sarah, Sarah, Sah, Sah, Sah.'"

I had a puppy once, I had a brother, I had a man, and a daughter. And I killed all of them. From the dog, I kept the bravery, from my brother the sadness. Jak-Ur gave me the rage, and from my daughter, I kept the skull. And as I ascend to the hill to meet my destiny I carry only a few more things with me.

Listen to me, you all, Jak-Ur, father, brother, priest, Crispus, Khun-Taa, all of you who came to reign over me. I will not run and hide, that decision I made long ago. I made a promise to my little brother that I will fill wells with the blood of this tribe. All things happen for a reason, all the sinners and the believers will be judged, so the priest always said, and he read it in the Book of God and who am I to doubt God? You will be judged, today.

It was for a purpose that I learned every word, Legend, and Story of your tribe. Our Tribe, now. I had the witch give me the herb that makes the voice coarse and wise, and I chewed on it, like cud, for years. For a purpose. I had a reason: to be the first woman south of the river who can shoot this bow, Enaka's bow that I strap on my shoulder. To suffer years of pain lifting my child up only with two fingers. And I don't plan to kill anyone with this bow, I could, but that's the weapon of the many.

I have other weapons, much more powerful. "Hunt a wolf for me, my love. Bring me his hide." I've torn my dress, above the waist, my breasts are naked under the gray wolf-hide, as I ascend to the hill. There is a reason I chose this hill, the one across the Blackvein River, the one that the full moon will rise from, and my shadow will shine in the full Selene, atop the hill, above your camp, my leader, great Khun-Taa. *Look up, I command you.* Look at your First, because I will be your First, I was Sarah, and I will be Sah-Ouna the First, see the long skull of my daughter that I hold in my hand, still burning my fingers in the chill of the night, it will burn forever, that murder of the innocent I will have to live with. *Live. If what I have left is still called life.*

Ascend, Khun-Taa. Ride your rose gray stallion; I am waiting for you at the top of the hill, see my breasts in the half-open wolf-hide, awaiting you full and eager. The trader brought me a good razor, and I shaved my head, and I threw the black hair down the well. I am a witch and an archer, a Storyteller and a mother of a Longskull, I am your Goddess. See me shooting the double-curved bow, aiming at Selene, hear me sing the Legends of our Tribe, I'll talk to you about our ancestors and the she-wolves, about Khun-Nan and Ouna-Ma the First, I'll tell you of cities, princesses and Gods who await you to ravage them, I'll whisper to you of Reekaal and dark forests. Don't ask, you know where I come from, Enaka has sent me, my Khun, you cannot doubt that, if it was just the songprayers and the bow you might, but not the skull. Once you see the quiver skull of a child, you are mine forever. Don't ask who I am, because you know I am her voice. I was sent by her, the one who sacrificed her children to save us, our one and only Goddess Enaka, I was sent to guide you, to sing to you your destiny. Drink the lolum I boiled, my Khun, venture with me in the darkness, let me sing to you the Story of the First Reghen, let me take you in my mouth, and bathe with you naked in the moonlight. It took me seven years of pain and sacrifice to get here, I made a promise of revenge, you don't need to know any of that, let me tell you the Story of Khun-Taa's father, the one that only you and a few Reghen know, and Jak-Ur, one of the Rods who heard it long ago from your own lips. Believe. Don't doubt; I am sent by Enaka, my name is Sah-Ouna, I used to be Sarah, but no more, and I am your destiny.

Don't whimper, my Khun. Not yet.

Butterfly

XIV.
The Legend of Nothing

Thirteenth Winter. The Sieve. Twenty-Eighth Night

"Only seven lashes? He was easy on you," Rouba told me.

I had asked him once. He was the older Guide and should know.

"Why Elbia? She was so… She was the best."

"That's why. They chose only her from the entire Sieve. This and forty-one other camps," he said. "What sacrifice was worthy of Enaka? That weasel Atares or that worm Ughi? Or should we have offered the Goddess the ashes of a ninestar like you? The curse had to be broken, Da-Ren."

Rouba motioned to a child, a Carrier, to bring more manure for the fire.

The sickness stopped spreading a little while after Elbia's death, exactly as Sah-Ouna had foreseen.

"And if it hadn't stopped, Rouba?"

"We would need another sacrifice."

It was so simple, and I understood it many winters later. After some sacrifice the plague would stop. Exactly as Sah-Ouna had foreseen.

Bako was spreading a different, false story: that Elbia was the one who had brought the curse to the Tribe and had to die. As much as I wanted to split his head in two, my strength had left me. Even from then, early on in my life, I understood that I wouldn't be able to split open all the heads that spat out stupid stories.

"Rouba didn't tell you the whole truth. I will tell you why they killed Elbia," Malan told me on the twenty-third night after seeing me alone and lost in the darkest corner of the tent. "If you give me your meat today."

"Half."

He turned to leave when I stopped him, offering the meat in my hand. I had fought all day to win it, only in the hope that I would learn something from the Ouna-Ma's Story. I picked it up from the mud and the piss of the fallen and washed it in the rain. When he ate it, he looked at me with a grin and patted me softly on the shoulder a couple of times. His lips were tight and his head was nodding.

"I will tell you. When you're older."

I jumped on him, and we punched each other until Keko's lashes split us up. I got most of them because I wouldn't stop.

I could feel the fresh wounds opening with every movement for many nights. My lips were torn and swollen, and that was a good excuse for me not to eat or talk to anyone. On some days, I stood through the trial because I could forget the pain. On others, I just didn't care and fell. Not on purpose. Atares's fate didn't find me.

The only thing I cared about was to escape. The Forest on the north and west sides of the camp was a dark world I wouldn't enter. To get to the trees, I had to get past the maulers. And then, what would I do in the trees? Reekaal lived there, wolves and terror.

Most of the sheds with the hay bushels were on the eastern side. Everyone would see me if I climbed over the sheds. And then to get down, I would have to jump above the wide and thorny bushes. The easiest way seemed to be the most straightforward: escape from the southern gate, the one everyone used.

I waited one night when I had purposely fallen. I was at the last tent, the one at the farthest southeastern point next to the gate. Our Guides had left us and gone to their own tent for shelter. A drenching rain was falling, the kind that washed out scents, footprints, and sounds. The children around me were asleep. Most of them had passed out. I kept my eyes open. When one of the children moved in the middle of the night, as if to wake up, I hit him from behind with a wooden pole and he fell back down.

I crawled outside and made it to the only gate. No one was guarding it. I would leave and never come back. I didn't know where to go. Maybe I just wanted to make it easy for them to send me to find Elbia.

I got out of the camp easily in the night, but without torch and stars, the only thing I could do was feel my way around in the mud.

But I was free and away from the Sieve.

I slowly started to see a few flashes of light in the rain. I was in a clearing with tents all around. The flashes were escaping from the small gaps in the tents that were burning dung fires. I saw three more tents beyond the clearing. Six tents were in front of me as I dragged myself along the mud road, the one used for carts and horses. I crept toward my left and came upon some sheds with hay bushels. I was in a second camp. Exactly the same as my own.

I continued south. I wanted to get somewhere, to find a horse. I came to a second gate, same as the one I escaped from. My hides, my skin, the rain, and the mud were all one. I passed through the second gate. I saw flashes from six tents in front of me on the mud road, three to the right farther beyond the big clearing, sheds to the left of me.

When fear and madness dance together, mortals can only laugh bitterly. Where was I? No matter how long I dragged myself in the mud, I was in the same place. I came to a third camp the same as mine.

"There are many camps like yours in the Sieve," I remembered the Reghen saying.

I sat under the shed to rest and clear my head. As if Elbia could hear me, she pleaded with the Goddess to part the clouds of Darhul that were hiding Selene. Rain puddles caught the moonlight and glowed faintly like ghostly torches. I could now see more things but they could see me too.

I was in another camp. Different from my own. But the same in every way. And I had just passed another one. Also the same. I reached the easterly tent in front of me. I could make out from its position that it was one of the Sheep's tents. I looked inside. A fire. Smoke was escaping from the hole. Many children. Twelve-wintered like my peers, they seemed. Madness was dancing faster than fear.

I climbed to the top of a shed. I looked toward the east to see what was beyond the thorny bush. More camps. Identical camps, like giant cages everywhere around me. I got away only to find them in front of me again. I jumped down and started to run back to my own. A dog barked somewhere behind me but didn't follow me. Running in the darkness, I passed the entire third and second camp and finally made it back to my own. Just before I stepped into my tent, Keko came out. With squinting eyes, his head bent to the right, he called out to me, "What are you doing here, orphan?"

It took me three breaths to answer him. Then I remembered that I had fallen with the Sheep the evening before. I had to carry out the chores of the camp for the first time.

"I am a Carrier tonight, I'm getting to work," I answered.

"In the middle of the night?"

"The fire. Inside. It's fading."

He let me go.

I hid into my tent. The fire inside was indeed fading. And so was hope.

The thirtieth day of the Sieve found me a Carrier. In grief and shame. I wished to have the plague, to be done. I didn't have it.

Instead of Elbia, the Greentooth waited for me in my dreams on the thirty-second night. She was kicking me in my sleep and saying, "Buckets, wake up, fill and carry." It hurt.

Someone was really kicking me. It was Rouba. "The Reghen will tell a Story tomorrow. Don't miss it," he said.

"About Elbia?" I asked.

He shook his head.

"I don't believe this. You are really doomed, you know. Yes, her too," he mumbled, his eyes looking away from me.

I wanted that Story. If I could just think of nothing all day, nothing but the Story, my legs would hold. They did. On the thirty-third night, in the winners' tent, I looked to find some hope again in the Reghen's Story. Something to help carry me forward. With my belly full of meat, the Reghen began his Story for yet another night, one of the last of the Sieve. We had been through a whole moon and were almost through another half.

The Legend of Nothing
The Fifth Season of the World: Part Three

There was once a Drakon, blue as icy death and gray as sorrowful life. He had one less than ten crystals for eyes, legs like ancient frozen trees and ice needles bestudding his scales. He protected the river's crossing to the North and had sealed the passage to any living creature. The Tribe had to cross the river or perish, and Khun-Nan asked, "Who is brave enough to go and kill the Drakon?"

"I am!" shouted the First Reghen, the fastest of the three identical brothers. "For I can turn backward on my saddle and lie down on my chest, and with my horse in gallop, I can shoot nine arrows, each only a breath apart, straight into his nine eyes. And then I can pull in one move both blades from their scabbards and send them straight into the beast's heart."

But the First Ouna-Ma, the daughter of Khun-Nan, answered, "Another will be needed to help him."

And Khun-Nan asked again, "Who else will accompany him?"

"I will," answered the Second Reghen, the strongest of the three identical brothers. "For I can defy hunger and cold, and climb for days, and walk for nights in the snow. I will find the Drakon's lair and wait, for as long as it takes, until he falls asleep. And then I will tell my brother to come."

But the First Ouna-Ma answered, "We will need yet another."

And Khun-Nan asked again, "Who else will accompany them?"

And the Third Reghen, the wisest of the three identical brothers, stepped forward and said, "I will also go, my Leader, because the Drakon is a sly demon, and he will set a trap for my brothers."

"And what can you do?" the Khun asked.

"Nothing!" replied the Third Reghen.

"Nothing? What good will that do?"

"When I wait patiently in the icy cold for two nights, what do I fear? Nothing.

And when I have nothing to eat for three days, what do I wish for? Nothing.

When I empty a quiver of arrows, what distracts my mind? Nothing.

When the othertriber begs me for his life, what torments my soul? Nothing."

And the Ouna-Ma answered, "Now they are enough to defeat not only the Crystaleyed, but all the Drakons."

And so it happened.

The Second Reghen, the strongest of the three, left on his own and searched for two moons. It was he who found the Drakon and led the others to the demon's whitest lair, white of the snow, white of the crushed bones.

He waited awake for nights, and when the Drakon fell asleep he signaled for the other two to approach. But the Drakon fooled them, for his nine eyes never slept all at once. One of them was half-open. The Drakon spread his wings and chased the Reghen with the rage of forty winters.

"Run to save yourselves," shouted the Second to his brothers.

The Third Reghen was ready.

The Second had done his duty. Now it was up to the First, for he was the only one who could kill the Drakon.

The Third had only one thing to do. Nothing.

The Third did not run. He stood still in front of the Drakon. The beast flew over the frozen river to attack him. The distance between them closed. The raging fire from the monster's nostrils surged around the Reghen's shield and scorched his face.

The First Reghen, who had climbed and hid among the white hair of a willow tree, found his one chance. He aimed as the Third was burning in agony. His iron-tipped arrows flew and shattered the crystal eyes of the Drakon. His iron blades tore through the air and sank deep in the beast's heart. The ice river boiled in the Drakon's black and green blood.

The three Reghen brothers returned victorious, though the Third was disfigured for life. He wore his gray hood so as not to frighten those who looked upon him and never took it off again. His brothers, the other two identical Reghen, also wore their hoods to honor their own.

The Third, the Reghen of Nothing, had very little life left in him. A treacherous ice needle had found its way into his body when the Drakon got close to him. The ice needle grew and grew next to his heart until, by the next winter, it had pierced his lung and sent him to Enaka with the most triumphant of Stories.

The two brothers Reghen continued to wear their gray hoods, eternally loyal to the Third. They never took them off.

We defy everything.

We sacrifice the best.

With our sacrifice, the entire Tribe we protect.

We fear Nothing.

Or else, and far worse, we die for Nothing.

Thus declared the Ouna-Mas, the Voices of the Unending Sky.

All the children, except for one, hypnotically repeated the Reghen's last words of the Story: "Nothing. Nothing."

The strength returned to the Tribe in the days to come, and to the children. We did not hear any more coughing. The curse had been lifted, and the dying no longer breathed near the same fire with us. As the days of the Sieve were running away, the children took the Reghen's words and made them a game.

"It will rain all day today."

"What are you thinking, Bako?"

"Nothing."

"When you fall and there is no meat at the Sheep's tent. What do you think, Urak?"

"Nothing."

"The maulers have come for the orphans again. What are you thinking, Malan?"

"Nothing."

"What are you thinking about, Da-Ren?" Rouba asked me on the thirty-eighth day as we were walking toward the Wolves' tent yet again just as twilight clutched the last clouds in the west.

"Noth…"

Nothing. I couldn't see her smile.

"Noth…I…Elbia," I answered.

Rouba stared at me silently for two breaths and then slapped me on the cheek, trying to wake me up from the nightmares.

"The snakes have gotten your spirit, kid. Elbia would have understood. It had to be that way. Elbia has risen in glory, up in the stars. We ended the plague with her blood and with her body. And her eyes cry with shame for you every time she sees you losing yourself. You disgrace her."

"Her eyes did cry that morning, Rouba, but…"

It wasn't shame.

"And what do you tell her, acting like this? That she died for nothing? Death strikes fast. No begging, warning, explaining. That is the Sieve."

That was the Sieve. It wasn't enough to have strong legs and never fall.

We had to endure three trials, to face the three deaths as they had told us from the first night.

Cold.

Hunger.

And the third, the unspeakable, the most terrible.

I hadn't tamed the third yet, the tyrant of despair, of Nothing, to be able to stand again and endure after losing all light and all hope. When Nothing would matter anymore.

We did not bury the dead in our Tribe, but that night I buried Elbia into the dark past and moved forward.

To Nothing.

Apocrypha VIII.
Harvest the Innocent

As the One Mother heard the Legends, Chapter VIII

North of the Blackvein there are no months or years. Time is the slave of Enaka and her daughter Selene. The men count the days by looking up in the sky, when it is not cloudy, the women count the moons until they give birth to sons again, unless they are archers or witches. I am the only one who is both.

Some names are easy to guess, the flower moon, the snow moon, the strawberry moon, the antler moon, the hunter's moon, the longfish moon—what they call the river's blackfish with the fire-colored eggs. The harvest moon. They don't work the land or harvest it; the harvest moon is when they raid the south and the Empire, early in autumn before the rains. Rain kills the horse, and the bow, cold is no time for war, neither is scorching heat. The mares are rested and well fed when the harvest moon starts. They harvest the innocent, as they harvested my village.

The worm moon is the one when I am most powerful, the moon of the First Witch, the one when I still light a candle for my brother, the first of spring. There is a great feast every spring, and they all kneel to me, waiting with teary eyes until I bring them the Voice of the Sky.

There are so many of them, north of the Blackvein, the ones who call themselves the Tribe, as if they are the only tribe of men, and everyone else is slaughter-meat. They are afraid only of the Forest and the Witch, and I rule as I knew I would, by stepping on their fear and their Goddess. I had a brother once, now I have thousands of brothers, and they all kneel to me.

It took some time, though Khun-Taa was my slave from that first night. I was never confused, never doubted myself. I was amazed at their numbers, and by their savagery. Jak-Ur couldn't count or explain. I thought this was a tribe of thousands, but I never guessed more than two thousand. I had no understanding even when they crossed the river, following Khun-Taa and myself. Not until I crossed the river north after the raids to see Sirol for the first time. Only then when I saw the thousands of campfires, did I understand what I was up against, how strong I needed to be. This tribe can end all life, raze the living from the face of the earth; they are Satan's monsters, not the scourge of God as the priests of the Cross call them.

Countless the hooves and the boots that will crush the skulls and the sepulchers, sow fire and salt, so that no life will ever sprout again. Those first moons made me wise; I saw the rape of my village repeated a thousand times farther south. I saw my face and that of my brother and mother in all the faces of the innocent. I've seen too much I can't describe, the lard on the stakes, the boys begging, the crucified mothers. I've seen so much, that I cannot doubt my mission or cower now.

I wailed at night alone, as my Khun slept next to me, drunk and exhausted. I woke in the morning with rage to lead the sacrifices, to cut the heads off the priests, one more time.

I am a hater and an unbeliever, and yet they all kneel in front of me. It is essential for a leader to have some hatred for his own tribe. Else how can she lead them forward, sacrifice some to save the others, separate the wheat from the chaff? It is essential for a leader of any faith to be an unbeliever. Else how can she make up new sacred stories when the old ones become useless?

One thing I learned is that whether one is unbeliever or faithful, we all walk through hell.

It took me six bloody moons of tales, kisses, and soft words before I made Khun-Taa listen to me. He listens to the prophecies now, and I have stopped them. One woman alone.

I ordered them back north of Blackvein, I prophesied his death in the south, and Khun-Taa doesn't cross the river anymore. He doesn't dare go west, either, and there is nothing in the north. I had to draw blood, to lead the sacrifices with the blackhorn knife, else they would never fear me. The few slaughtered ones come in my sleep to haunt me, but I saved thousands farther south, thousands who never saw me, yet they curse my name.

This tribe feeds on war and horse and rots in peace and mud. I keep them in Sirol, isolated and tamed, to drown in their Legends of monsters and fear. One day, after they rot and become weaker I will drive them back to the steppe to die deep in the desert they came from. And they will follow me with song and milk-spirit, that bitter piss they drink. I would be done by now if only they had wine.

I can't kill them with fire and blood, but I will one day end them all with wine and song and a prophecy they'll fulfill with teary eyes. I don't do this out of kindness; I am not the sword of the Archangel that descends to avenge God. I have become rage and revenge; I hate weakness, I crave the power, the young longskull girls who surround me and listen to me, the Packs of the Archers looking up at me at the Great Feast of Spring, the twelve-wintered boys and girls of the Sieve. I must judge them, sieve them and decide their fate. Make no mistake; I admire this tribe as much as I hate it. I might bring the end of this tribe, but I would never live anywhere else, never leave them.

There were many women around Khun-Taa when I first came, many more beautiful than I was. By the time I found him I had a shaved head and weary eyes. But a woman spreading her legs, and showing her full breasts, that is not power. It can save her life for a few nights, but it cannot bring her to rule a tribe of monsters. It takes a lot more to accomplish that. A few could. The blue-eyed one I cursed and exiled to the Forest because he was mesmerized by her. The one from the north, the brown-haired one, I ordered her death, and yet I still fear her child, that orphan. He came to life nine days after the Great Feast of Spring. That night I dreamt of a priest and a rag doll at the edge of my bed. They were laughing at me and out of their mouths came a river of spiders. I marked the newborn of that night, the ninestars, to remember them forever.

It has now been thirteen winters since Khun-Taa found me up on the hill, twelve since I became the First Witch.

Short after giving birth to him.

The one who will be Khun, my seed, the greatest Khun of all, the one whom I bred to lead them to their demise.

Even his name I chose to foretell that, but they are too stupid to recognize it. Stupid and vile. And I am their First Witch.

It is his time now, his Sieve.

The Last Day

XV.
Crazygrass

Thirteenth Winter. The Sieve. The Final Night.

No one fell on the thirty-ninth day.

"Tonight, everyone is a Wolf," said the Reghen, early, with the first light of dawn, before we even undressed.

Whispers traveled from mouth to mouth that the Sieve would end that very afternoon or the following morning. And then what? I could no longer remember my life before the Sieve. But all trials come to an end someday. The worst trials of my life ended when they were finally under my skin and I had accepted them. As brutal as the trials were, by the time they ended I feared what followed more.

Some, like Bako, were bragging that they would join the Archers and leave for new trials and glories away from us shit orphans. They considered themselves the Wolves of the Sieve, even if they had fallen many more times than I. Before Elbia's death, I had fallen only once. I fell a few more times after that twenty-first day. I was no longer the best, whatever the best could mean.

Unlike Bako, I had no idea where I wanted to go. It would be enough that I wouldn't return to the Greentooth. The weakest began to pray to Enaka. But it was their prayers especially that she wouldn't heed.

The Guides ordered us to light big fires in the middle of the field, and we brought hides to sit around. When the Sun was high, the Carriers passed milk to everyone. Not meat, and that worried me. But the maulers had disappeared, and everyone believed that we would leave at once. No trial awaited us.

"Today is a feast," said Keko.

Rouba was pacing, caring for the horses. He never sat down to enjoy the fire.

"It's not over," he said when he found me for a moment alone. "Keep your eyes and ears open. It begins now."

We lit seven fires in a circle. Five of us gathered around each one, with a larger fire in the middle for the Guides.

Beyond the field, to the west, I saw them. Skeletons taller than any warrior, holding hands, frozen white, wearing only the gray hair of a mad witch on their skulls. They weren't marching, but they kept waving at us. I kept looking until I realized that they were nothing but snow-covered oak trees, their branches white on the side above, gray-dark below. Once more, the Forest disappointed me.

Nothing had come out of the Forest that winter. No animal, monster, or man. Only howling and leaves. When it wasn't snowing and the sun was shining, the wind would bring us the only message of the Forest. Bronze leaves would lift up from the earth and dance all the way to reach our camp. Bronze was the only new shade the Forest brought in a Sieve that was colored scarcely. Black, gray, brown, white. Red.

I was looking for the Reekal of the Forest. For the Wolfmen I'd seen that eighth day. I never told Elbia about the Wolfmen. Why? Maybe because I had never wanted to worry her. Maybe the Wolfmen were another one of my dreams. As I was looking west to face my fears, everyone else was looking in the opposite direction. A cold wind embraced me as if Elbia's ghost had glided past my body, coming to join the festivities of the Sieve. Sah-Ouna had just passed the gate and entered our camp.

"She has come again, Da-Ren. Careful now. It isn't over," I heard the ghost whisper to me before it hid among the oak skeletons.

Sah-Ouna was not alone. A younger Ouna-Ma was next to her, the one I would call Razoreyes. When she took off her red veil, I forgot about Elbia for a while. I learned then to create nicknames for the Ouna-Mas and the Reghen to tell them apart. She was the same as the rest. Black hair cropped short like wet grass, black pupils reflecting the endless darkness of the Sieve and the long quiver head. But her eyes were different, younger, and sharper. Razoreyes.

I didn't fall in love with that Ouna-Ma, nor did I touch her. Not then. Winters later, when I got to know many Ouna-Mas, their tongues, their breasts, and their legs, then I fell in love with all and none of them. I didn't have any feelings for Razoreyes. Only the feeling of something growing hard under my trousers for the first time.

"They come out from the womb that way. They were born wrapped within their mother's womb sheath, still unopened."

It was Bako talking close to my ear, which was enough for me to know that this was all nonsense.

"The pupils are like that from the herbs that they drink," Rouba told me.

"When they are still babies and their skulls are soft, the older Ouna-Mas tie their heads with bandages, and that's how their skulls get their shape," said Danaka.

I believed her. A girl can't be blinded by a razor-eyed witch. We boys were already moths doomed by the merciless blaze of her eyes. It was us boys whom Enaka and Sah-Ouna desired. They prepared us, countless boys, to suck our blood and marrow in the Final Battle.

Denek, who was frequently in the Sheep's tent, said the pupils could grow twice their size and cover almost the entire eyeball when they fucked and reached ecstasy. I didn't know then what he meant, but as I grew older I saw it many times. And I learned that it didn't matter. Whether they were born or became that way. The Ouna-Mas carried the Story of the entire Tribe, the past and our future. Their power came from us.

Razoreyes and the Reghen sat next to Sah-Ouna as she began reciting the sacred rites. A cauldron was already on the fire. I had heard the Guides cursing whenever cold, rain, sickness, or death came. I didn't know what these swearing words meant, but they were at the tip of my tongue.

"What do you want with the cauldron, you vile bitch, you Darhul's vomit? Do you want my beating heart, to throw it in there? Do you want to rip my eyes out so that they never see what they saw on the twenty-first day? What demon are you to sacrifice Elbia?"

I didn't cry out the words, nor did I whisper them. Why should I? The Witch knew my every breath. She knew what was eating me inside. Enaka knew too. We were not hiding in the tent but outside, under her Sky, where no secret could be kept. At the edge of the western horizon, the Sun wielded his bloodied swords, fighting Darhul in the last battle of the day. Who was I to argue with the mothers and the daughters of the mighty Sun himself?

The Witch took out some herbs, a rasko root, and some dried walnut leaves and threw them one by one into the pot. She never touched the walnut leaves with bare hands but held them with a cloth. She then carefully took out from a pouch a small branch that looked like wheat in shape but was green in color.

From a distance, I saw Rouba's mouth open and close many times, saying the same word over and over, but I couldn't hear what it was. Rouba was whispering, "Crazygrass," but I understood that later. The pot boiled fast, and Sah-Ouna filled a cup and took four sips four times, turning the cup to the four points of the horizon.

We had remained outside all day, and it was now dusk. Razoreyes was passing around a cup of crazygrass to all children. She passed it around four times, refilling it from the pot. After the third sip, my head was burning and my fingers were ice cold.

Sah-Ouna took out of her pouch a skull, small, like a child's, but long as a snake's egg. She placed it next to her. A Guide brought her a sack, and she pulled out a white rabbit, still alive. Sah-Ouna took the rabbit in her arms. She looked at me. When I looked at the rabbit again, its neck was broken. It trembled its two last breaths and then its limp head fell to its side. She took out the ritual knife with the black handle, its blade shining over the fire.

"The blade was forged under a full moon by six one-eyed naked brown-skinned Blacksmiths," said Bako.

For some reason, I believed him this time.

Just three nights ago, the moon had been full.

Sah-Ouna began to sing in a low, mesmerizing voice. It was not a song, more of a spell. Again and again. She said the words nine times.

I do not take the life from this rabbit;
I take the darkness from the tent.
I do not go to death like a sheep;
I go to my wolfen ancestors as a friend.
I do not take the blood from this animal;
I take the fear from your blood.
I do not throw the lola into the pot for you to lose your minds;
I throw the lola for you to find the memory of the old world.

The Witch made a small cut and pulled back the rabbit's white fur from the top to its two hind legs. She broke its joints and then skinned the rest of the animal's body and its head. The fat white rabbit now looked like a skinny rosy rat. She cut off the bushy tail and the head and opened the belly.

She took out all the entrails with care so as not to break the shit and piss inside. She held the heart and let it fall into the fire. The rest she gave to Keko, and he threw it away. I heard the maulers.

As Selene proudly rose, Sah-Ouna went into a trance that grew deeper with every breath. She fell backward and her eyes turned, becoming as white as the rabbit's fur and the children's faces around me.

The Guides brought more skinned rabbits ready for roasting, one for each fire. They cut each animal into four pieces and roasted them skewered on sticks. The Guides made us drink another sip of crazygrass.

The Reghen gathered the sticks with the rabbits' heads and placed one in front of each tent.

"To keep away the night demons. They always come on the final night of the Sieve to take the Sheep," said the Reghen.

Razoreyes took two knives and began to dance with slow movements, bending her knees and waist in warrior positions. She circled the still body of Sah-Ouna and cut the air above her with sharp moves. She had an otherworldly beauty, this Ouna-Ma. For many nights in the winters to come, when I thought of a girl, Razoreyes, slicing the air with two blades, came second in my mind. When I grew older, I dreamed of her dancing around me. Until one day, after a few winters, that too happened, and she did dance atop me.

"What is she doing? Why is she cutting the air with her knives?" I asked.

I wished she would open Sah-Ouna's throat and suck all the blood of the First Witch.

"She is protecting the body of the First so that no demon wind ghosts enter her."

"See, Sah-Ouna is weak now; her sister has to protect her," Danaka added to Bako's words.

I wanted to scream, "Where in Darhul's name are all these demons? All I see is a witch slaughtering us."

As if he had read my silent question, the Reghen started his last Story of the Sieve and freed all the demons in the tent, mixed them up with the crazygrass we had drunk, and sank us into a nightmare before we even closed our eyes.

The Legend of the Final Battle
The Sixth Season of the World

You will know when Selene becomes red like the bleeding heart of the Goddess and remains that way for four moons. This will mark the time of the Final Battle, the Battle that will destroy this world. And so will end the Fifth Season, that of the Khuns of the Tribe.

The only being that existed before this world, the Demon Darhul, will rise with his nine heads from the sea and drag his hideous body onto the earth one final time. There, on the spring flowering earth, he will go to battle against the Only Goddess of the Unending Sky, Enaka. The servants of Darhul will be:

...to the North the Crystaleyed Drakons with the ice needles on their scales. They die only from the sleep of forgetfulness. We must never go back, or we'll awaken them.

...in the South the Deadwalkers, led by the treacherous Sorcerers, the Priests of the Cross. They hide in underground caves marked with crosses and crawl beneath the earth. They dress their half-alive corpses with clothes and jewels and swords. Even if you put them to death, their priests resurrect them from their bones and their rotting flesh. Only fire or beheading can annihilate them.

...in the West the deadliest of all, the bloodeating Reekaal, those who block our way forward. By day they sleep within walnut trees, and by night they feed on the blood of warriors and children who have wandered astray. The walnut trees bear fruit in the shape of small skulls, and within them are the brains of their doomed victims. Never go near them.

In the Final Battle, they will surround us and raise massive stone walls around us to stop our brave Archer riders. Mountains will spew thick smoke and choke the Sky. The Sky will cry a black poison that melts flesh and stone. The earth will burn hot, the ice castles of the North will melt, and the Drakons will bring their fury south. No one will be saved.

Then Enaka, in her flaming chariot, will descend for the last time to Earth with a thunderous crash. All who are ready will drink from her strength, and our warriors will be unleashed on the four corners of the Earth. And neither from the East nor from the South nor the North will they be able to stop us. In the West, there where the Sun kneels every night, the Final Battle will take place.

Archers of the Sieve, you are the sons of the Goddess, the ones to fall and rise in glory in the Final Battle.

Our sole ally in this battle will be the gray-haired Wolfmen, the servants of Selene, our ancestors and protectors. They breathe each night next to our sleeping young in the Sieve. They take and devour the weakest among us to preserve the strength of the Tribe. And if we lost a few of our comrades in the Sieve, we shall remember that the Wolfmen have commanded it.

You will be grateful to them in the Final Battle. When Darhul rises in front of you with his twice nine times burning nostrils that will spew out the End, a coward is not what you will want at your side.

Thus declared the Ouna-Mas, the Voices of the Unending Sky.

We had eaten better than any other night. We had drunk worse than any other.

"Wolves…devour the Sheep…in the West…Final Battle… Razoreyes…"

For a poisoned child losing his mind from Sah-Ouna's boiled crazygrass, I could remember quite a lot. But not enough. I had forgotten the songspell of the Witch, the one that began with "I don't take the life of this rabbit," and that would cost me everything forever.

I dreamed horrible dreams. Maulers with bat heads and pitch-black eyes had formed a circle around the field, and I was in the middle of it lying helpless. Blood poppies grew out of my mouth, the four-legged creatures licked my naked skin, and the Ouna-Mas were sucking my strength. Razoreyes passed her forked tongue through one of my ears and out the other.

I awoke on the last day, the fortieth, just as I was starting to choke on my vomit. The Sieve was over. Almost.

XVI.
One Will Lead, All Will Fall

Thirteenth Winter. The Sieve. The Final Day.

Most of us couldn't stop the water running out of our asses all night. I was lucky enough only to vomit. Three times, and then I could stand again. I always had a strong stomach, another gift of the Greentooth, who fed us whatever was filthiest on this land and below it.

At dawn, the Guides found us awake, shitting, and moaning. As I stepped out of the tent, I noticed that the number of Guides and horses had doubled. My head was pounding as if the horses were galloping in there with iron hooves.

Keko and Rouba shouted for us to line up in the field.

"Dressed."

Rouba stopped me at the horses' watering trough.

"Drink water for five horses. The nightmare from the crazygrass kills," he said.

I fell to my knees, puked one more time on the frosty earth, and then grabbed the trough with both hands. I dipped my head like an animal and drank. Rouba pushed me back.

"More. Clear your head. You will need it today. Today is your whole life's Story."

The children were in line. They put me first to the left, and the Reghen said, "Last day for all of you today."

A few smiled. Most kept moaning. I looked at the ones smiling. The Sheep always smiled for all the wrong reasons.

"All in one line, you follow him," Rouba pointed at me. This jolted me out of my daze. "Da-Ren, you're first. Start walking. There."

I lowered my head and squinted. We hadn't gone *there* ever before.

"There," he showed me again pointing northwest, toward the Forest.

To my right, the sun had risen pale and weak, just like the day he devoured Elbia. *Sacrifice?*

I started walking toward the skeleton oaks.

"Where are we going?" asked a boy behind me.

"Where everyone bleeds," answered Keko loud enough for all to hear.

No one was in front of me, not even a Guide, as if I knew the way. The fog was shrouding my path in a white gloom. The trees were emerging slowly through the mist, one by one, as I approached them.

Elbia told me a Story before the twenty-first day. She said there was an age-old bloody war going on in the Forest every night, every winter. The firs and the oaks were fighting. For many winters now, the firs were winning. Their trunks standing strong spears of darkness, their branches rising up black and green iron blades. The oaks were withering away. Their branches thin like the bones of the weak, their trunks gray, wrinkled, and old. The oaks were bleeding death. Their blood, a bronze river of leaves, was crackling under my boots.

"But how can the war go on every winter if the oaks die?" I asked her.

"They come back. In the spring, they rise again."

It was the last Story she told me. I wanted to ask her but never did, "Are children oaks or firs?"

I kept a steady pace among the bronze path of leaves. It felt like I was completely still and the trees were floating toward me. The bats were sleeping through the long winter. The first birds of the dawn were the only life on the branches. A handful of redbreast robins and starlings with shiny feathers, green and gold like the Forest of spring. The morning dewdrops were sprinkling me from above, trying to help me.

"Wake up, Da-Ren. It's the last day."

I could hear her voice warning me, and when I closed my eyes I could see her ice-blue lips. Crazygrass.

I took a wrong turn when I thought I saw her shadow among the firs. Rouba ran forward and showed me the way. His face, worried, brought me back.

"Why am I leading?" I asked him.

"Malan at the back is asking why he is following," he answered. "Shut up and move!"

Rouba walked next to me, mumbling the songspell of the night before.

I do not take the life from this rabbit;
I take the darkness from the tent.
I do not go to death like a sheep;
I go to my wolfen ancestors as a friend…

Senseless words. My head was still pounding hard from the crazygrass.

Not much later, we reached a glade. I saw a ring-shaped field about eight times my fingers in paces from one end to the next. The field's fence was made from poles thrust into the ground and tied together with rope. There was an opening to the fence, a gate marked left and right by two spears like the ones the Rods carried. On the opposite side from where we were standing, there was a second opening of the fence. It led to a square tent.

"A red tent!" Bako cried.

It was a square tent with dark stripes. It was too far to tell whether it was red or black. Just dark. The stripes were painted uneven and violent, wide in the middle, thinner at the edges, as if the nails of a monster had clawed at soft flesh. Our tents were all round. Very few, like those of the Ouna-Mas, were square. Even fewer were painted with the blood-red stripes, and no one ever went near them.

"If you want to live, do not ever enter a red-painted tent," said one of the well-known Stories of the Tribe.

"You get in but never out of a red tent," added another boy, a Sheep whose name I still didn't know.

"So, is this the Endless Forest?" Matsa asked.

"This is a small woodland, not even the beginning of it," said Bako. "The Forest starts half a day's ride from here. That way." He pointed west.

We stood there for a while, still trying to remember Stories about red tents.

Urak saw them first and let out a cry. Outside the red tent, two shadows as tall as men, walking on two feet. They had the head, the fur, and the tail of a wolf. The Wolfmen that I had seen on the eighth day in the Sieve. This time, everyone saw them. There were two of them.

They were quite far, so I could make out their shapes but not their faces. One of the shadows turned toward us, crouched down, and let out a long howl. Robins flapped their wings, and starlings shat their green and gold feathers.

"I told you. You didn't believe me," said Bako. The fool was happy that the Legend was true.

Some of the children were already running back to hide in the trees but didn't go far. The Guides chased them and gathered all of us in front of the fence. We all huddled close, touching. A couple were holding hands. We were not a long line anymore but a bunch of scared sparrows. Or starlings, or robins. I looked around. I tried to listen. All birds had disappeared.

Danaka said, "This is a cursed place of bloody rituals. I've heard of this. The last day of the Sieve. The Wolfmen. They take the weak."

We were all there, weak or not.

If I hadn't gone through the madness of the Sieve, if I hadn't been poisoned by the crazygrass and the Reghen's Legends, then I might have seen clearly. I would have seen two tall men dressed with the hide and head of a wolf. Because that was what I saw after all. But that morning, none of us saw men dressed as wolves.

We were all sure that we had seen two fearsome otherworldly monsters. Wolfmen. The Guide said, "We'll all bleed." The Wolfmen shadows were howling, the tent was painted red.

"Look there—more of them," said Danaka, and my head turned right to the woods.

At first, they did look like a pack of black monsters walking toward us, their heads coloring the mist blood-red. But as they came out of the woods, I recognized the red-veiled Ouna-Mas approaching on foot. Reghen and Rods were also coming along with the Witches. Warriors followed them as well, on horseback. It was the second time the warriors had come to the Sieve to see us. Maybe that was the fateful time for me.

"Is she there?" I asked.

"Shut up, Da-Ren," Keko said.

Malan pointed at the pack of the Redveils. There was a black veil in the middle. He didn't talk, but as he was looking at me his lips made silent her name, "Sah-Ouna."

Malan was as calm as the Blackvein's water.

The Redveils and the rest came up to the fence and took positions as if they expected to watch something. Sah-Ouna was not in front, I couldn't even see her.

"Trial. Not sacrifice," I heard again Atares warning me. His voice was coming out hoarse and cold. I turned but didn't find him. Atares was long dead. A mauler had ripped out his throat. Crazygrass.

"Urak, you're first. Get here!" shouted Keko, who stood close to the fence's opening. Urak didn't move. Two Guides grabbed him and took him to the middle of the field. He was there all alone, about six breaths of fast running from where I stood in the fence. Short and angry as a mauler, strong and stupid as an ox, he started to whirl around. Everyone stared at him. Rouba threw him a small knife and pointed toward the center of the field. Two small sacks were there. Urak approached them, hesitating and stopping every few steps.

"Hey, Urak, watch out. Darhul's head is in there," yelled Bako, ending his words with a nervous laugh.

Cowards laugh when scared. Rouba smacked him hard.

"You don't get to laugh today. Watch. Stupid!" said Rouba. He might have hit Bako, but he was looking at me when he said the words.

Urak opened one of the sacks slowly and stuck one hand inside. The sack moved. He let out a scream and pulled out his hand. He was bleeding. A white rabbit jumped out of the sack.

Malan laughed. But Malan didn't look scared. I should have laughed too, only because it happened to Urak. But I was busy trying to remember. Something familiar. Sah-Ouna just the previous night, the songspell, the rabbit.

"Rouba was right. I should have drunk more water."

I was talking to myself. I had no one to talk to. Elbia and Atares had gone to the stars, Malan rarely spoke, and Danaka and Bako were not ones I wanted to have words with.

Urak was always the stupidest of all of us. That's why he became a ravenous beast when he grew up. The rabbit was out of the sack on the ground. Urak and the rabbit stood still and stared at each other. The beast made the first move and started to chase the animal. It was already too late for him, and the rabbit disappeared with quick leaps outside of the fence.

Urak jumped over the fence to chase the rabbit, but the two Guides, one of whom had lashed me many nights before, caught him and dragged him back into the field.

"A second chance," said Matsa.

The Guides didn't stop in the middle of the field. They kept dragging him toward the red tent. His legs were now in the air. He was kicking and screaming, trying to walk backward as they dragged him.

A Reghen shouted, "Three."

All the Reghen together shouted around the field, "Three."

The children around me were breathing hard. The Guides threw him into the tent but stayed outside.

I heard Urak scream three times far and across from the other side of the foggy field. The first scream was sudden as if he had just seen a Wolfman in front of him, the second was a short shrill like a trapped bird, and the third was a drawn-out bleat like a lamb in slaughter.

We heard, we didn't see. Then silence.

Danaka had come next to me. She squeezed my hand.

"They bring the piss-carrying orphans to have meat for the dogs," she had said to Elbia on the second night. I pulled my hand away from hers.

They brought four more children, one by one, for the same trial. Some I didn't even know. *Sheep* or *Carrier* were the only names I called them. They had the advantage of knowing beforehand what was in the sack. They had a knife. But they all failed to do the simplest thing in the world. Some didn't even manage to catch the animal, and none managed to break its neck, skin, and disembowel it. That's what we had to do, what Sah-Ouna did the night before. Everyone tried to do that without asking, without being asked to. They had given us a knife, we had to kill something. Something weak. Knife, prey, kill. Simple. Wrong.

The Reghen were shouting after each failure: "Three," or "Four."

Kuran was sixth in line. Everyone knew he was born ill-fated. He'd come out of the womb with a dense black tuft of hair growing on the palm of his hand. Maybe they were right about him. He picked his sack, put his hand in fast, and pulled it out faster. There was no rabbit, only a black scorpion walking away from the sack. Kuran was holding his hand, screaming in agony, his face between his knees, crying in the middle of the field.

The Reghen shouted, "Four."

They dragged him to the red tent.

"Shit! Now I have to worry about which sack to pick."

I was still talking to myself, but at least I was fully awake now and making sense. I had to keep my head clear. Knife, prey, kill. That was all.

Another doomed child chose the scorpion later, and then it was Matsa's turn. He was the first who succeeded in breaking the rabbit's neck but failed at skinning the animal. His hands were trembling so much that he couldn't skin the thing. He grabbed the knife and started hacking at the rabbit until it became a bloody, hairy mess. The Guides grabbed him.

The Reghen shouted, "Two."

I looked at Malan. He had a grin and made a helpless gesture with both hands open. Matsa had lost it. Malan was enjoying this. The screams from the tent continued, always coming from the last child. We never heard more than one child at once. As if all the previous losers had been silenced forever.

Danaka spoke to me. "Do you think we all end this way?"

"No, I don't," was the only thing I said.

Six times the fingers on my hand I counted the children who had gone before me, and all of them failed and disappeared amid the terrible screams of the red tent. Everyone else around us—Guides, Ouna-Mas, Reghen, rabbits, and scorpions—remained silent.

That was how Danaka too was lost from my side.

When Bako failed, we heard his screams louder than any other, even before he entered the tent. And a little after.

Malan and I were the last. Sah-Ouna, who until then remained invisible, approached the fence, and the space opened around her.

I suspected then that we were not given our turns at random. Malan, Bako, and I were the strongest. We had feasted more than anyone else in the Wolves' tent. Elbia would have been with us too if she were alive.

"Let's get this over with," I said, not silently.

I was ready and angry as a bowstring pulled. If I could just keep my hand from shaking. If she could help me choose the right sack. I'd seen her only that morning among the firs. Dead-white skin. If only I could forget all the other losers before me, their screams piercing my skull. They made it seem so much harder than it was.

I cast a last glance around and saw that many more warriors had gathered. The Ouna-Mas were around Sah-Ouna. Their black robes all clustered together looked like a great beast, their veils adorning it with a garland of red flowers. And there was Khun-Taa, our Leader, on his long-necked warhorse. I had seen him once before, and it was enough to remember him. My legs sank into the ground as if all these horsemen were standing on my shoulders.

What had they come to do? To watch children who can't kill a rabbit?

But my turn had come, and there was no breath left for another thought. I searched for Rouba and found his gaze. He clenched his fist to give me courage. He wouldn't talk, but his lips whispered, "Nothing."

Nothing to fear. Nothing would stop me.

Keko pushed me into the field. I was walking toward the sacks, and the earth was hard under my boots. I wore boots, unlike the previous days. I reached the sacks, and right away, at an impulse, kicked the one to the left. I had learned that much in the Sieve: a cunning mind was rewarded. I kicked something softer than a rock, probably the body of an animal. A cry, like a baby suffering. I had found the right sack.

I turned to see if anyone would stop me, but no one made a move. So many Redveils, Archers, Reghen. Malan was the only child left to watch me. He was looking at me, grinning and moving his fists up and down in rhythm. As if he were cheering me on.

I let out a deep breath and tried to keep a clear head. "I must not lose the rabbit." I opened the sack only slightly enough for my hand to slip inside. Even if it cut my fingers off, I wasn't going to let go. I took it out of the bag. It was soft and white as snow. I held its warm neck for a few breaths. I heard a purring sound and its teeth clicking. We were calm now. Happy. Both of us. I squeezed. It scratched me a couple of times, but I couldn't break it.

It turned out afterward that it's really easy to break the rabbit's neck. Hold it belly down with one hand on its neck, grab its hind legs and pull them back in one fast move with the other hand. If only I had watched her more closely. She was a witch. I thought she could break the neck with her eyes only. That's what witches do. They fool us. But I didn't know how to break its neck. I needed something else—a club, a knife. I had a knife. For skinning.

I knelt, grabbed my knife, and held it under the rabbit's head. My blade was cold. The rabbit made a funny growl. Its eyes were blood red. It knew; it was time. I slit its throat. A brief tremor. My hands warmed red.

The evil beast, the little snow rabbit, was dead. Life became prey, warmth became trophy, pouring became food, fear became victory.

I had to skin it now, but that was easy. It was food. Food doesn't make any sound or movement. I started to skin it first from its blood-red belly and then along its back. I had dressed and undressed many small children in the orphans' tents. I threw out the entrails. The animal, skinned, was slimy, and the morning's vomit taste came back at the bottom of my throat. I carried on with a frozen mind. I had forgotten all about the tent. It wouldn't see me. I thought only of the animal and how I would devour it roasted that night.

Just as I was about to finish, I heard murmuring. Next to the gate was Rouba standing, staring at me tight-lipped and disapproving. The Ouna-Mas were under their veils. The warriors were shaking their heads. I had done something wrong, but what?

I stopped looking at them and fixed my eyes on the rabbit. It took a few breaths for me to figure it out. I had thrown away the entrails, I had a skinned rabbit, but I did not have a heart. I stuck my knife into the guts and nailed the heart up with the knife. With my other hand, I grabbed the skinned rabbit and then lifted my arms in the air.

Cheers and battle cries rose around the field, loud enough to reach all the way up to the Unending Sky.

Did she hear them?

The rabbit's heart was small and dark as a ripe olive.

"Bring me a fire to throw this heart into!"

I said that with the thunderous voice of a thirteen-wintered boy who had conquered the whole world. They were still cheering. There, with my two arms raised in the air, victory's cry coming out of my very soul,

I let out the first of only two tears of joy that I was ever to shed in my entire life. I made it. Even if the stars had foretold otherwise. Even if she couldn't see me anymore. At least she would hear me.

I took my rabbit, and with one push I thrust it onto one of the two spears that marked the fence's gate. The Guides let me walk out of the field. Rouba's hand slapped me on my back and threw me to the ground. A wide smile carved deep wrinkles on his face, deeper than ever.

Malan was the last one, but there was no glory left for him. I had stolen the thunder of the day. At most, he would just do whatever I had done. Maybe he would kill the rabbit with his hands like the First Witch had, but what more could he do? I didn't know what the victor would win. Another piece of meat or his life outside of the red tent? But I was the one.

Malan passed two steps away from me and walked slowly, head down into the field. Not once did he look around him, his eyes fixed on the sacks. He grabbed one sack, without hesitation. I saw something move inside and knew that it was the rabbit sack, but he didn't seem at all concerned with it. With his knife, he stabbed the other sack and walked away, leaving scorpion and blade behind.

He turned around and came back toward the fence, where I had speared my rabbit. I was right there.

As he came face to face with me, he whispered, "Oh no, Da-Ren! You killed it."

"What?"

He had the eyes of a Reghen, naked of fear or joy. He pulled my rabbit, dead and skinned, out of the spear and threw it into the same sack with the other one. The skinned rabbit embraced the living one in the darkness. I still remember this as the most savage moment of the entire Sieve. If they'd had souls, those rabbits would search for him in the nights.

"*I do not take the life from this rabbit,*" Malan whispered only for me to hear.

I did not understand what he was mumbling, but I was already seeing his back. He was walking away from me with the sack. From the spear to the red tent on the other side of the ring, he made steady steps, eight times the fingers on both my hands. He didn't look to the left or to the right, he didn't gaze at the sky nor at the ground. He reached the entrance of the red-painted tent holding only a sack with two rabbits and no knife.

The warriors were murmuring again. And it was louder now. Khun-Taa was too far for me to hear him, but he kept pointing to the red tent and Malan and talking to the Rods around him. Some Ouna-Mas lifted their veils. A medley of whispers and cheers grew with each of Malan's last steps, as if Darhul were rising from the waters of the dark sea.

I turned my gaze to Sah-Ouna. She had lifted her black veil. She wasn't looking at me. She was looking at Malan, who was almost outside the red tent of the Wolfmen. The Witch was trembling like a child, and tears ran down her pale-white cheeks.

Malan pulled the hide flap away and went into the red tent.

"What was that? What did he do?" I asked loudly, but no one was paying attention to me anymore.

The warriors' horses came closer to see that which their riders couldn't believe, and I held from one of the poles so they wouldn't trample on me. I was the only little one there.

No matter what I did or how loud I was asking, no one noticed. I looked for Rouba. He was looking away from me, toward the tent. From Sah-Ouna to Khun-Taa himself and the Guides, all cheered and pointed, wide-eyed. As if they had seen a demon walking on earth.

Sah-Ouna made a signal for silence. Everyone obeyed. The wind came sharper and colder. Not a sound was heard, nor any screams coming from the tent, though I thought I heard a wild roaring laughter. Reghen and Rods were pushing me backward as they moved in front. I couldn't see anything. I slipped from in between the horses and got to the front again.

"You—what are you doing here? Get back in the field." A Guide was talking to me.

Then I saw them coming from the opposite end of the field, in one line, like a sad herd of sheep that the mist had spat out. Urak, Matsa, Bako, Danaka. And all the others. Keko was leading them. I ran toward them.

They had bloodied rags wrapped around their arms, but none of them was bleeding badly. They were walking on their own. All were still alive. Very much alive. They passed in front of me and looked at me, one by one, with a questioning look as if they were asking why I wasn't with them. Why did I not have a bloodied rag tied to my left arm? Their eyes kept looking backward as they passed me. They aligned next to me on the fence within the ring. Only one was missing.

Malan came out of the red tent. His hands were empty, no sack, and he was walking slowly with his head held high toward us. He reached us and took his place next to me. No Guide stopped him. His left arm was not bloodied. He wore no rag like all the other kids. We were the only two still uncut.

Sah-Ouna entered the ring of trial. Once again, I thought she was coming for me. Once again, I was wrong. She was close enough for me to feel her breath, but it was not blowing on my face. She wouldn't turn her eyes toward me. She put her hands on Malan's cheeks. They were both shaking as if they were burning coals and Malan was an Ice Drakon. She knelt and her hands extended to touch his face and begged to the Sky:

Sun, come out to see your offspring.
Brave, our blood has tamed the night.
Wolf, hunger, Selene, arrow.
One will lead. All will fall.

Farther away, from the direction of the red tent, unnoticed by most, came two strangely dressed men, laughing. They were wearing wolfskins on their heads and their backs and around their waists. They even had two bushy tails tied behind their waists, and each was carrying a rabbit in his hands. One skinned, my rabbit, the other freshly killed. The two rabbits Malan had brought them. They took off their wolf hides and looked the same as all the other Guides.

I pointed to Bako so he could see them.

"Your Wolfmen. There!"

He saw them long before I did. He already knew there weren't any Wolfmen. They were the men who had bled his arm in the red-painted tent.

The Guides and the Reghen had taken care all these many winters of the Sieve to create this deception. The last day, a foggy day, always foggy. The Wolfmen standing on the other side, next to the red tent, far away. They were walking and crouching in a strange way that confused me more than the skins they wore. Howling. Dressed as Wolfmen were two towering Guides, taller than any man we had ever seen before.

The First Witch walked past me, ignoring me completely, and stepped out of the field. I knew I had lost then, because Sah-Ouna did not sing for me. It would take me many winters to understand what was at stake that day. "My whole life's Story," Rouba said at dawn.

"All the children of the Sieve, move to the center of the ring field. You will now meet your fate!" shouted the Reghen.

No one had left. All warriors were still watching from their horses.

The Reghen began to recite his last words:

The Truth of the Last Day of the Sieve

Listen all to the commands of the Goddess of the Unending Sky. This is the last Truth of the Sieve, and you will henceforth carry it on this land until you return to the stars.

Through the trees of the misty Forest crept the eternal Demon Darhul and reached the field of the Sieve. His talons big as fir branches; his green breath fouled the air. He smelled the fear of the weak and carved them deep twice and thrice, some even four times.

The carvings of the Demon and of your shame are on your left arm tonight. Other carvings will come in your life, and each will mark your cowardice.

The weakest of you will leave here now, the last day of the Sieve, with four straight marks carved. You will never be warriors. You will become

Hunters, Fishermen, Blacksmiths, Tanners, Craftsmen. You too are men of the Tribe. You too shall be worthy because the Goddess wants everyone at her side. But you are not warriors.

If you leave here with three lines carved, take care not to receive a fourth. You must remain throughout your further training and life with three carvings. And if you do so, you'll become warriors, honored and star-born. But you will always obey those who have fewer carvings.

The few of you who will remain with two carvings after your training of five springs are worthy and strong enough to become Pack Chiefs. You may one day have forty warriors behind your horse at your command.

Those with only one carving, you are proud sons of Selene, fierce leaders of men tomorrow, counted on the fingers of one hand, and Enaka favors you. If you remain this way through your next training, you can become Leaders of a Banner and command many Packs and all their Chiefs. The Banners of battle are only five, and you are one of a kind. With only one carving, you may lead all the Archers, or Blades, or Rods, or Craftsmen, or Trackers.

Listen, all. In battle you will give your blood under the banner that Enaka has chosen for you. If you live to become so old that you can't carry your blades to the battle and need to rest your weary bones at your glory's winter, you will get five carvings and join the old Guides.

Thus declared the Ouna-Mas, the Voices of the Unending Sky.

Khun-Taa on horseback came nearer and stood silent next to the Reghen. Up close he looked old. Old like Rouba. His eyes were sunk deep into the cave of his skull, his left arm bare and uncarved, a gray wolf's fur covering his back and the right arm. There was the mark of an awful gash on his face underneath his left eye. He had escaped Darhul's talons, but some othertriber's sword had found his flesh. Countless winters ago, he was a child walking in the same Sieve.

The Reghen continued:

"Today, many of you received your first carvings of shame, but you will receive even more as you grow. You will leave for training for five times spring. Do not shame the Goddess and the fate she has chosen for you.

Listen carefully now, and as soon as you hear your names, go behind the Guide who carries the banner of your new fate. You see the Guides with the banners of the Archers, the Blades, and all the others waiting to your left. You will go there tonight, to the banner Enaka has chosen for you. There you will find your peers from the many other packs of the Sieve, and a lot more children, older than you, novices. You will train with them and the new Guides who await you there.

This is the Truth that the Sieve has carved:

Kuran: Four Carvings—Fisherman

Denek: Four Carvings—Tanner

Ghera: Four Carvings…"

I was looking for every face that the Reghen named. Kuran was not even listening, as he was still in agony from the scorpion's sting. But his torments had ended. For the rest of his life, he wouldn't have to face anything wilder than the salmon jumping out of the Blackvein. I was the leftmost except Malan, and they were all passing in front of me before they went to their new banners. Denek, the Tanner trainee, came out of the line, dragging his misery. He had untied his rag from his arm to see it again, as if he couldn't swallow the Truth. Four carvings on his arm, deep and bloody, one under the other. Bako yelled at him as he passed by, "Keep a warm pair of trousers for me. My balls are freezing!"

Denek didn't pounce on him. He never had. He was not a warrior.

The fates and the names continued. As soon as the Reghen called out a name and I looked at the child who stood out, I could immediately foresee his or her new banner and the carvings he or she deserved.

"Urak, three carvings—Blade.

Danaka, two carvings—Archer.

Matsa, two carvings—Archer.

Bako, one carving—Archer."

The Reghen stopped calling out names. Only Malan and I were still standing where we started. The others had moved behind their new banners. It was almost noon, and the fog was still breathing on me like an old and sick winter demon between my legs. A different Reghen, the oldest I'd ever seen, came forward. His voice was different. Grim. I still waited for my name. There were no carvings on my left arm. The old Reghen spoke. *"And if…*

And if…oh Goddess, you brought such an honor upon us again today…

If any of you leave here today Uncarved,

without even one iron's scratch on your arm,

you, who escaped the talons of the Demon,

And didn't kneel in front of his stare,

then,

then after your next training, at the westernmost camp of the Uncarved,

then,

tomorrow you might become the Only one, the Sixth, the One Leader of the Tribe, the next Khun.

And if you are here in front of us, have pity on me, my Khun, that I have still not recognized you, my next Great Leader, if in front of you I uttered dishonorable words.

I kneel in front of you, Uncarved. One of you will be the one who will lead us tomorrow in the Final Battle with Sah-Ouna on your left and Enaka on your right side."

The Reghen went silent. He looked at Khun-Taa. The voice of our Great Leader, deep and loud, filled the field like a rusty old blade that still yearned for a fight. That was all that came out of his mouth.

"Da-Ren, Uncarved. Malan, Uncarved."

Those were the only words that Khun-Taa spoke in the entire Sieve, and the Reghen continued, "You two, Uncarved, follow the Guides with the Wolf banner. They will get you to your horses."

"Your horses." I repeated the words to believe them. I walked behind Malan toward the last banner, the one orphan of children. The Reghen turned also toward the Guides and the children and spoke. "You have all faced the three deaths of the Sieve, and now the hard training begins for five times spring. If you succeed, you won't be marked again. Enaka waits for you in the Final Battle. Prepare."

I had won, even though I was born an unlucky ninestar.

Elbia, Atares, Ughi, Rido, and many other children whose names I never learned had fallen. They were resting peacefully in the Sky above. Except for Elbia, the *blessed* sevenstar. I was sure that I had seen her that morning, as I was walking among the firs and the oaks, a solemn ghost blending in with the mist of the Forest. She was whispering to me, "I promise you, Da-Ren. We'll ride the war horses together."

Kuran would gut fish for the rest of his life. Denek would rub skins with fresh horse piss to remove the horse smell. Danaka and Matsa could become Pack Chiefs, leading up to forty warriors. Bako could even become the Leader of the Archers, the greatest warriors, countless of them. Our best warriors under his command. I hoped that the Goddess and Khun-Taa would not be stupid enough to ever make that mistake. Someone, somewhere, older, younger, definitely smarter, with only one carving, had to exist who was better than Bako. Urak would never become anything more than a cutthroat in the Blades and would never command anyone.

No knife had come near Malan or me.

After forty dawns in the field of the Sieve of the twelve-wintered, the Reghen, the Ouna-Mas, and the Guides decreed that I could become the One Leader of the Tribe one day. Despite the red triangle that still marked my fate and my skin.

But Sah-Ouna had not sung for me, and everyone cheered for Malan. I had lost, because...because I had done what I was told to do? It didn't make sense. My mind wasn't helping me. For one moment, I had won when I held the precious black pebble, the rabbit's heart, in my fist. I had lost.

Denek and I were the two who stared with the eyes of defeat.

I parted with all of them without goodbyes, except one.

"Forget it," Rouba said as he came close to me just as I was mounting my horse and becoming taller than the whole world. It had been almost two moons since I had ridden, even for a short while.

"This is my fifth winter in the Sieve. Not one has ever done what Malan did today," said the old man.

And that was the balm to soothe my soul?

The darkness of defeat cloaked my heart. Not for a few days. I repeated two words countless times till the end of my days in Sirol. Every morning when I woke, if I didn't say them in the morning, I would say them a little later. These two words that were born orphans in my triumph.

"I lost."

Many times, every new day.

We all headed north under different banners. The woodland we entered in the morning had ended, and we were in open fields again. The path took us even farther away from the camps of the Sieve. The other children left on foot. For a little while, we could see them behind us; then Malan, the Reghen, Keko, and I trotted faster. My group kept a northwest direction toward the Forest. Every other banner turned east. I would not see the other twelve-wintered for a very long time. I was alone, once again.

My mind kept bringing back Sah-Ouna's words. How she ignored me. I started making up Stories in my head to find some solace.

"It is all a lie. It is unfair," I said to myself. There were signs for everything, they told me. I had read them. Sah-Ouna favored Malan, and she told him what to do. They cheated me out of my victory.

I was riding last not because I had lost, but because I so much wanted to stab Malan in the back, even if it meant they'd put me to the stake that same night. Sah-Ouna had favored him and cursed me. I kept repeating it inside my head, poisoning myself more and more each time. It was not helping. He had slowed down and was riding close to me. I spoke the words loud enough for all to hear. "The Witch had told you what to do."

Malan looked at me with narrowed eyes, shaking his head left and right, before he decided to reply.

"That is true. She told me exactly what to do," he answered. His voice was calm. The veins in my head swelled, like the waters of the Great River in the early spring.

Keko was riding in front of us. He had given Malan the banner of the Uncarved, the one painted with the head of the wolf to carry. He himself had five carvings and was forbidden from carrying such a heavy banner of the Tribe.

The Reghen drew close to me, grabbed my reins to stop my horse and to get my full attention, and said, "The rabbit was not the enemy. The red tent was."

I would remember it till the day that I'd die. If the Sun could turn around and dawn only one day again, to do everything differently, I would choose that day.

Malan slowed his horse so that he was right next to mine and said, "The Witch told all of us what to do. Don't fall asleep again when you are being spoken to. Tomorrow I will be giving you orders."

Malan kept riding a few feet in front of me. He was humming, singing. I had heard that song before. The Witch's songspell. The wintery wind took the words from his song and darted them, burning needles in my ears and frozen blades on my chest.

I do not take the life from this rabbit;
I take the darkness from the tent.
I do not go to death like a sheep;
I go to my ancestors as a friend.
I do not take the blood from this animal;

I take the fear from your blood.

I don't throw lola la lo la la la la lo lo la,

…the crazyweed will steal the minds from little girls.

"The words of the Selene Witch were wise and clear. She told everyone yesterday what to do today," the Reghen next to me added.

"What are you saying?"

"You got scared, Da-Ren. Ride forward. It happened to everyone," said the Reghen.

Malan started singing the songspell of Sah-Ouna again. He didn't stop repeating it for the rest of our ride. At some point, when I stayed far back so that I wouldn't have to hear him, he turned and grinned at me. He lifted his fists up and down in rhythm, one of them clasping the wolf banner. As if he were cheering me on.

For the first time, I really feared that I would never beat him.

Apocrypha IX.
Remember the Songprayers

The Lost Apocrypha of the First, Chapter IX

I kept you in my arms, sang to you for nights and days, I watched every step you took and sound you made as a small boy, and yet you remember nothing of me. It had to be so; if you knew that you are the seed of the First Witch and the Khun you would become nothing. A boy crushed under our greatest shadows. The Khun might kill you himself at your eighteenth. You have the dark eyes and pale skin, just like my twin brother.

You feel it; you know that this throne belongs to you by right and prophecy, by Goddess and Witch and Man.

I raised you among the red tents, the longskulls, the boys and the girls your brothers and sisters and ripped you apart savagely from them and me. It is that torture that makes a boy strong, I had to torture you to make you what you are, sent you to the Orphans.

But the winter of your Sieve has come, my love, my only child. Come tomorrow you will join the Uncarved, and one day you will become the One they all fear, the Khun. I'll make sure Khun-Taa ascends to find his Goddess when your time comes.

I watch you proud and cold, cold and proud; I can show no tear or joy at your brave deeds, else they will know. The Reghen are a monster with two hundred eyes, and they know the small things, the furtive glances, a tear withheld. I am always careful.

So ends your Sieve, my brave son, in triumph and glory.

I had a daughter once, a sister you will never know, as you will never know of your mother. I brought her skull to the tribe.

My son will be the next Khun, and he will make piles of skulls of his enemies and his subjects.

My offspring, so powerful, will rule the world.

I know now that you are the One, I knew the moment you stepped out of that red tent Uncarved and unafraid. Maybe you remember the songprayers I lulled you with, when you were a child, maybe it is in your blood. You cannot hide from fear, as it was in my blood.

I do not take the blood from this animal;

I take the fear from your blood.

Do you remember?

That brown-haired girl, on the twenty-first day, I had to get rid of her, I saw how you were looking at her, the envy and the desire, and she never had eyes for you. Envy is poison, being scorned as I was by Crispus is poison, and you must have none of that. That girl was strength, I saw my strength in her, and something else, even goodness, and she too would cast a shadow over you. We have to murder goodness, early on, else it will spread like a disease.

Da-Ren, I thought I'd kill him before the Sieve ends, but then I changed my mind. Da-Ren makes you stronger. I didn't have to do anything more, I fear this boy, but he will be a worthy adversary for you, you need adversaries to keep you strong. I'll keep my eye on him, but that boy was broken twice, once when he learned that he is a ninestar, one I will never favor, and then again, the morning he lost Elbia. He will doubt his own fate enough to become his own curse. I know a thing or two about men, I keep thousands of them under my thumb.

It is time, my son. Your time. I will fade away for a while; my Legend needs to subside for yours to rise. You will know none of all this; all my secrets remain with me, you will walk the path alone. I will appear only when I should, to carve your destiny.

"One will lead, all will fall."

Rise, my son, the Malicious, the Malevolent, the Malady that will befall them all.

My son, my Malan.

Rise.

But never forget the songprayers; they come back, come back.

The Story continues in
Drakon Book II Uncarved

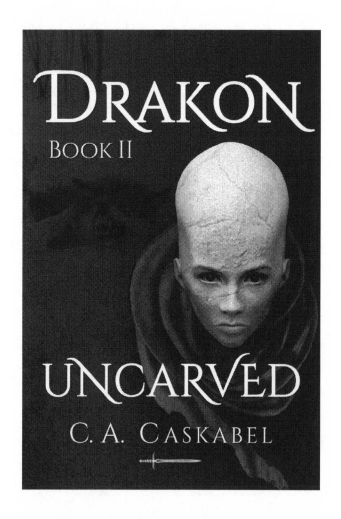

"How do the Uncarved die? They bleed to death. Always."

Fourteen-winter-old Da-Ren joins the Uncarved, the chosen few destined to lead the Tribe. More than forty children train and compete for the next five springs; only one will become Khun who will lead the fierce warriors.

Da-Ren's ambition and strength will keep him alive but can he overcome his most powerful and cunning adversary, the one favored by witches and men? The Goddess and the Ouna-Mas will try to nest in his heart, but is he prepared for the one woman he is brought up to hate? As war and hunger strangle the Tribe, the stakes of love, duty, and betrayal are higher than ever. A young man's first kill. A young man's first kiss. A coming-of-age tale with non-stop action.

Available Now!

About Drakon

Drakon is one completed story which consists of:

Drakon Book I: The Sieve
Drakon Book II: Uncarved
Drakon Book III: Firstblade
Drakon Book IV: Butterfly

You can find our newsletter, my journal and more information about the book at:

www.caskabel.com
journal.caskabel.com
www.facebook.com/CaskabelAuthor

Thank you for reading and reviewing

Till next time,
C.A. Caskabel

Join the Drakon Tribe.
Get the plunder

Join our newsletter to keep in touch with C.A. and win prizes. Those worthy (and lucky) will get their share of the loot! Prizes to be drawn:

- **eReaders**
- **Drakon Paperbacks**
- **Fantasy e-books (you choose)**

Click here to see to join this month's draw.

Join and Win
(http://caskabel.com/join)

About the Author

C.A. Caskabel started writing *Drakon* in 2013 and completed the 400,000-word epic fantasy novel in 2016. He split Drakon into four books which he will release within 2017, he promises. After all, he is eager to start working on the next novel. C.A. is also the founder of an indie publisher of picture books and fantasy fiction.

Before 2013, C.A. was a serial technology entrepreneur. He studied at Boston and Brown University. He calls Boston, New York, Providence, San Francisco, London, and Athens (and in general Planet Earth) home.

I'd like to thank

Editing: Aliki, Chris, Cheryl, Pete, Nick, Annie

Cover, Graphics: Chris, Dimitri

Website: Dimitri

Marketing: Constantine, Dimitri, Mihali, Christina

Production: Antoni, Dimitri

Everything: Liza

And many more friends and family for their support.

Made in the USA
Columbia, SC
23 January 2023

10900321R00140